A catalogue record for this book is available from the National Library of Australia
ISBN 978-1-7635635-9-9

Author: © Heather Anne Gordon

Title: Verses for Melanie

Acknowledgements:
We acknowledge and respect the deep spiritual connection and the relationship that First Nations people have to Country.
Country takes in everything within the landscape – landforms, waters, air, trees, rocks, plants, animals, foods, medicines, minerals, stories, and special places.
Connections to Country include cultural practices, knowledge, songs, stories, and art, as well as all people: past, present, and future.

Cover photographs: Heather Anne Gordon
mermaid mosaic on house wall

Internal design: Karen Marree Engel

First Reader: Jena Jaensch

Dedicated to Melanie Carter
feminist, swimmer, environmentalist, citizen scientist, activist, friend

Published by Centred in Choice
Sharing Australian voices, stories, strategies and skills with the world.
https://centredinchoice.com
PO Box 448 Alice Springs Northern Territory 0871
Australia

salt and soil

we honour the first peoples
of these lands and waters
their deep spiritual connection to country
country that holds land and sky and water
plants and animals
stories and ancestors

we pay respect to elders past and present
and to the generations rising
whose knowledge and care
continue to guide the tides

sovereignty was never ceded
this always was
and always will be

VERSES FOR MELANIE

mermaids live in the in between
where labels loosen
and the water forgets our rules

they are not half anything
they are whole in more than one way

they teach us
that difference is not deficiency
that belonging
does not require transformation

no one should trade their voice
for the right to be seen
no one should shrink themselves
to fit the shore

equality is the ocean saying
there is room for every current
and every body can float

HEATHER ANNE GORDON

This print edition
published in 2026 by Centred in Choice

Title: Verses for Melanie

Author: © Heather Anne Gordon
verses created 2020 - 2025

First published by Centred in Choice
ABN 17 601 690 975

Copyright © Heather Anne Gordon

these pages weave truth and imagination
the injustices are real
the mermaids are the metaphor
the tide is the call to change

dedication

to the women who flowed before us
the feminists of the first waters
the ones who learned to breathe
where breathing was forbidden

the brave ones
the tireless ones
the ones who slipped beneath barriers
and surfaced anyway

with salt in their hair
and resolve in their bones
they pressed their palms
against stone walls
until stone softened
until gates rusted
until the sea remembered itself

even when the world
cast nets and hooks
drew lines through water
named depth dangerous
named silence safety

they stayed with the tide

feminism is
our current

not a straight line
but a moving body
felt through scales and tides
through breath shared with water
through listening that travels
far beyond the self

our compass is not a point
but relationship
between stars and water
between mothers and aunties
between daughters and those
still shimmering into being
between the ones who walked before
and the ones entrusted to come

the southern cross does not rule
it turns
reminding us that guidance
carries responsibility
to wait
to move
to hold
to release

the milky way is not backdrop
it is law in motion
dark places speaking as clearly as light
ancestral paths still travelling
beside us
within us

the sea listens to the sky
the sky answers the sea
and we are held
inside that conversation

shimmering on the skin of water
the stars keep faith
with tides
with seasons
with those who read
with care

this is how we are guided
not by conquest
but by kindness
not by command
but by consent

before us
swam feminists
scaled and strong
who claimed the right to vote
the right to lead
the right to speak
the right to rise

into waters once closed to them
they carved sea paths
through silence
through fear
through generations of held breath

they shaped the seabed
with their bodies
their courage smoothing rocks
that cut them
so our bodies could pass
with fewer wounds

they worked as tides do
returning again and again
widening the waters
lifting girls and women
into fuller seas
into freer currents
into futures
once locked behind reefs

we honour them
with movement
we follow their wake
we swim because they swam first
we surface
because they taught us how

and now
as old storms gather again
as hard won waters
are drained and claimed
as depth is once more
named dangerous

we feel the pull back
reefs ripping
channels narrowing
old storms wearing new names

this book is one small song
in the long swim toward equality
a shell held to the ear
a remembering

feminism is needed now
as it has always been
because water forgets nothing
and neither does sky

this tide is for them
and for every girl and woman
swimming beside us
diving after us
or still far upstream

still glowing
like bioluminescence
in the deep

feminism is
the oceanic framework of our lives
a current we trust
a constellation rippling overhead

not a lighthouse of command
but shared orientation
a way of travelling together
through night

until equality
is not a distant shore
but the sea itself
the water we move through
every day

Contents

part one

mermaid writings

verses for melanie

we are here for the long swim
the deep tide
the slow river of verse
that drifts into the open sea
the crashing wave that refuses silence
the mermaids rising
through the murk of misogyny
hair streaming like sea grass
voices unbroken even underwater

australians

australians are born into a sea of misogyny
a wide restless ocean that we pretend is calm
yet even the surface ripples with prejudice
thin sharp lines of bias
skating across the top of the water

beneath that surface
currents coil with contempt and disrespect
disdain drifting like cold underwater rivers
scorn circling women in their workplaces
pulling at them tugging them off balance

and deeper still at the seabed
hatred settles like toxic silt
festered and heavy
sending up messages of violence
whenever women stir the water
whenever they create
small bright eddies of equality

some ask if this sea is exaggerated by feminists
some prefer not to swim too deep
some are afraid
of what they might feel in the darkness

but misogyny is real
a tide of prejudice and malice
a slow undertow of contempt
it is woven through our society

its definition flowing beyond the literal
past the narrow claim that it means only hatred
for the word has evolved like language does
stretching to hold all the ways
women are pushed downward
all the ways that power tilts and stays tilted

misogyny is a way of thinking
a way of breathing
that lifts men into primary status
that whispers entitlement into their ears
that binds women to the reef
limiting movement freedom possibility

and from this thinking springs conduct
a whole stormfront of abuse and control
rape and sexual offences
harassment and bullying
domestic abuse
swelling and breaking over women's lives
wave after wave

these attitudes
and the actions rising from them
are what keep us from real equality
make no mistake
hatred does exist

what is feminism

it is the belief at the heart of the heart
that women deserve full equality
social economic political
equal ground equal breath equal voice

it is the knowing that the world is not there yet
that there is distance still to walk
waves still to cross
for feminists and every advocate
who dreams of a world less hostile to women
less indulgent of destructive men
less willing to excuse their harm

feminism is the long patient reshaping
the slow carving of a gentler landscape
a place where women's pleasure is not forbidden
where women's freedom is not debated
where safety is not a privilege
where dignity is not a fight

it is the tide that keeps rising
even when pushed back
the determination to create a world
where women can breathe without caution
move without fear
live without apology

what is misogyny

it is prejudice and malice
it is contempt braided through daily life
it is everywhere in our society
even when the surface looks calm

some cling to the word's old bones
insisting it means only hatred
but the word has grown
as women have grown
it has stretched
to hold the common attitudes
the quiet behaviours
the everyday cruelties
that push women into lower places
that keep the old imbalance alive
between men and women
between power and its absence

misogyny is a way of thinking
a way of seeing the world
that crowns men as primary
that gifts them entitlement
that presses women down
restricting movement
limiting freedom
shrinking possibility

and from this thinking
conduct spills out like polluted tidewater
rape and sexual offences
harassment and bullying
domestic abuse hidden behind walls
a whole spectrum of control
dressed as normality

these attitudes
and the actions that rise from them
are the reason equality remains a distant shore
make no mistake
hatred of women does exist
there are men who call themselves incels
involuntary celibates sinking in their own
bitterness
gathering in dark corners of the internet
sharing poison
threatening women
and sometimes breaking into violence

this is misogyny
the undertow we are taught to swim through
the tide we must learn to change

ageing and the erasure of desire

ageing is allowed
but ageing desire
is forbidden

society grants older women
some space
but only if they surrender
their sensuality
their longing
their heat
their hunger
their erotic self

older women's sexuality
is treated as taboo
as embarrassing
as excessive
as grotesque
as something to be hidden
behind polite smiles
and quiet hobbies

desire is imagined
as a young woman's privilege
a currency
a performance
that expires
as soon as her body changes

the minute her hair silvers
her skin softens
her laugh lines deepen
the world decides
she is no longer
a sensual being
only a caretaker
a grandmother
a helper
a background character

the erasure is brutal
quiet
constant

older women
are not cast in love stories
are not shown in passion
are not imagined
as desiring
or desired
their erotic lives
disappear from screens
from books
from culture

as if arousal
has an age limit
as if longing
belongs to one body shape
as if pleasure
is something women
must surrender
once they become
invisible in the male gaze

but desire
does not evaporate
with birthdays
sex does not dissolve
into memory
passion does not become
obsolete

older women's bodies
hold histories
of touch
of pleasure
of discovery
of boundaries
of rediscovery
their sexuality
is wider
truer
more deeply lived
than youth ever allows

they know themselves
more intimately
than any young lover
ever did
they know what they want
what they refuse
what they savour
what they crave

and beneath the waves
mermaids silver haired
swim with power
with longing
with fierce erotic certainty

their tails glitter
with age
not decay
their bodies carved
by currents
storms
decades of movement
decades of knowing
how to feel

they are sensual beings
still
always
forever

their desire
has only deepened
as the tides passed
they claim pleasure
without apology
without shame
without hesitation

their silver hair
brightens the sea
their laughter
shakes the coral
their hunger
stirs the currents

while the world
tries to insist
that ageing women
must shrink
must quieten
must cool
must fade

the mermaids show
how wrong it is

they flirt with the moonlight
they dance with whales
they choose lovers
of any gender
any species
any season
they take pleasure
as a right
not a reward

older women on land
mirror this truth
secretly
quietly
in bedrooms
in gardens
in late night conversations
in reclaimed bodies

but they deserve
to mirror it loudly
openly
publicly
without punishment

their sensuality
is not shame
their longing
is not absurd
their pleasure
is not expired

and when society
refuses to see them
mermaids whisper
from the deep

you are still powerful
still wanting
still worthy
still alive

they rise
tails flashing silver
carrying this truth
to every woman
who was told
her desire
had an expiry date

they sing
you are not done
you are not invisible
you are not past anything
your desire
is your birthright

and no tide
no culture
no gaze
can take it from you

ageism and misogyny

in this sea of misogyny
there is a quieter current
a form of discrimination australia whispers
instead of naming
a tide so common
many do not see it at all
ageism

there is a mainstream belief
that when women reach a certain age
they pass their use by date
as if womanhood were milk
as if vitality had an expiry stamp
as if their time is up
and they must vacate the space
disappear
fade
become scenery
unless they are serving
caring
giving unpaid labour
to hold everyone else afloat

ageism clashes with everything
modern workplaces claim to value
diversity
wisdom
experience
merit
collaboration
yet all of these are dismissed
when the worker is an older woman
when the resume reflects lived years
and not only youth

where is merit then
where is respect
why is wisdom not valued
why is experience
the thing we celebrate in men
the thing we erase in women

diversity matters
not only because it is right
but because it creates the best outcomes
a thriving society is one with many perspectives
abundant lived experience
ideas from every age
every body
every shore

and yet
older men remain the mainstay
of television screens
our news anchors
our commentators
our public voices
wrinkles seen as gravitas
age seen as authority

but older women
become culturally invisible
treated as adornments until they are not
then removed from view
as if their existence disrupts the aesthetic
as if their bodies no longer suit the set

media shapes this
media amplifies this
and invisibility sinks deep
older women look and look
to find themselves
only to find nothing
mirrorless
self esteem eroded
not by age
but by erasure

how often
how truly often
do we see women in their sixties
in prime time slots
in starring roles
in positions of expertise
leading
shaping
speaking

age discrimination
is a monumental barrier
older women face doors closed
jobs withheld
opportunities shrunk

after fifty
the pathways narrow
income dwindles
options shrink
careers evaporate
as if only youth can generate value
as if longevity is not proof of skill

even language divides us
the casual use of boomer
turning generations into enemies
pitting young against old

instead of examining
the real structures
the real systems
that funnel power upward
toward wealth
toward whiteness
toward masculinity

to combat ageism
we must change perceptions
not only society's
but older people's own
teachings that age means decline
burden
slowing
fading
must be dismantled

ageing is natural
a positive life stage
a continuation
not a diminishment
older people are not burdens
they are knowledge keepers
story carriers
community anchors
essential members of society
with capability
creativity
and value that does not vanish
with each passing decade

older women
deserve to be seen
deserve to be respected
deserve to inhabit the world
without apology
without shrinking
without being smoothed out
or hidden
or dismissed

in these waters
the older mermaids rise
silver strands glowing in the current
tails strong with years
voices rich with depth
the ocean reveres them
for it knows
that wisdom grows layer by layer
like shells
like reefs
like tides

age is not the ebb
it is another swell
another season
another chapter

and the world will be changed
by the women
who refuse to disappear

beauty standards and bodily autonomy

beauty in this world
is a cage built slowly
layer by layer
adornment by expectation
a cage disguised
as aspiration

appearance becomes currency
before girls can spell
their own names
their bodies assessed
ranked
judged
dissected
long before they understand
they are more
than surfaces

fatphobia arrives early
sharp as a hook
teaching girls
that softness is failure
that fullness is shame
that hunger is a moral flaw
that shrinking themselves
is virtue
that occupying space
is sin

ageing becomes forbidden
lines policed
skin examined
hair monitored
natural cycles reframed
as decline
as disorder
as something to correct
to hide
to reverse
as if time itself
is a trespass committed
on women alone

cosmetic surgery pressure
rises like tidewater
marketed as empowerment
while feeding on insecurity
selling transformation
as salvation
changing faces
to match a single template
decided by men
refined by capitalism

consumerism whispers
fix this
lift that
erase here
smooth there
be desirable
be perfect
be profitable
be less you
more product

hair becomes politics
skin becomes hierarchy
features become battlegrounds
racism woven into every ideal
colourism etched into every standard
textured hair demonised
dark skin devalued
cultural features erased
to fit white beauty
white comfort
white aesthetics

bodily autonomy dissolves
under all this scrutiny
girls and women taught
to see their bodies
as public property
open for commentary
evaluation
intervention

and still
they are blamed
for caring
blamed
for conforming
blamed
for resisting
blamed
for existing

beneath the waves
the mermaid's body
is scrutinised too
even though she lives
beyond the shore

men invent tales
of her perfect tail
her impossible waist
her glossy hair
her smooth scales
her alluring face
stories that reshape her
into male fantasy
rather than sea truth

the mermaid becomes
the blueprint
for unattainable beauty
impossible proportions
inhuman symmetry
a body made mythic
so women
can be measured
against the impossible

yet in the deep
the mermaid's real body
is powerful
functional
scarred
strong
fluid
alive
nothing like the myth
that cages women

her scales shift with age
her hair tangles
in storms
her skin changes
with temperature
her muscles built
from survival
not aesthetics

she lives
beyond the logic
of the shore
beyond mirrors
beyond comparison
beyond the male gaze

but even she
cannot escape
the stories told
about her body

stories men wrote
not to honour her
but to control
the image of womanhood
for centuries to follow

yet mermaids refuse
these myths
their bodies
are their own
their autonomy
absolute
their beauty
unmeasured
unrestricted
uncommodified

they return
to human women
the truth stolen
from them

that beauty
is not morality
that ageing
is not failure
that fat
is not shame
that hair
is not hierarchy
that skin
is not destiny
that autonomy
is sacred

and women
are remembering

appearance as currency
is a lie
a trick
a system

and every refusal
to participate
every reclamation
every celebration
of real bodies
is a revolution

in the deep
mermaids sing
a chorus
for every woman
who dares to exist
without apology

you are more
than what they see
you are more
than what they measure
you are more
than what they want

you belong
to yourself
and that
is the truest beauty
there is

climate grief and gendered survival

climate grief arrives
like a slow rising tide
a sorrow that thickens the air
that coils in the gut
that wakes women at night
with the weight
of a burning world

women carry
the responsibility of climate anxiety
as if it is an inheritance
passed down through generations
of caretakers
gardeners
water watchers
fire survivors
foragers
nurturers
healers

they carry it
because they always have
because patriarchy expects them to
because someone must
and because women know
with bone deep clarity
that the earth is not separate
from their bodies

they are the ones
who manage the household during storms
who comfort frightened children
who ration the food
who track the weather
who know the land intimately
who see the first signs
of dying ecosystems
while men in suits
debate profits

women lead climate action
organise community gardens
lobby governments
educate neighbours
challenge corporations
protect sacred places
march in the streets
climb on machinery
stand before bulldozers
offer themselves
as the last line
of protection

and yet
they are the ones
who suffer first
and suffer most

when the river floods
it is women
picking up the pieces
when drought hits
it is women
rationing meals
when crops fail
it is women
who go hungry
so children can eat
when heatwaves surge
it is women
caring for elders
for babies
for sick relatives
with no respite

climate disasters
are gendered
and always have been

the burden
lands on the shoulders
of those already bowed
by unpaid labour
by economic insecurity
by domestic violence
by caring roles
that never end

and beneath the surface
mermaid activists rise
their oceans warming
their reefs bleaching
their kelp forests dying
their homes collapsing
into silence

mermaid activists
swim through waters
that feel unfamiliar
too hot
too acidic
too empty
too quiet

the fish are fewer
the currents confused
the songs of whales
fade
the coral cities
crumble into white bone

mermaids gather
to warn the surface
they rise
with grief
with urgency
with knowledge
older than human memory
but the world ignores them
dismissing their alarms
belittling their warnings
calling them dramatic
calling them hysterical
calling them mad

the same words
used against women
for centuries

climate grief grows
as fast as the temperature
the sorrow
of losing ecosystems
species
seasons
of watching water lines climb
and forests burn
and skies choke

but grief
is also a seed
a call to action
a tidal force
a refusal

women
and mermaids
are learning
to turn their grief
into uprising
into community
into resistance
into stewardship
into visions
of a world healed

they are the ones
who understand
that survival
must be collective
that resilience
must be shared
that hope
must be built
like a reef
piece by piece
life by life

and in the deep
mermaid activists
swim alongside them
carrying the memory
of every tide
every storm
every cycle

their grief
is not surrender
their grief
is a map

a reminder
that the world
can regenerate
if humans
choose to

and women
are already choosing
leading
healing
protecting

they refuse
to let the earth
be collateral damage
they refuse
to let climate grief
be the end
of the story

because grief
held collectively
becomes movement

and movement
becomes change

cost of being a woman

in this churn of economic misogyny
there is another current
the cost of being a woman
a cost paid in dollars
in hours
in futures
in choices
in exhaustion
in shrinking margins

feminists have fought for generations
for gender equity
but women not only earn less
for the same work
they also pay more
for the same life

the pink tax
a quiet drain
a lifetime leak
sometimes disguised as market logic
but always rooted in misogyny

until the first of january twenty nineteen
australia taxed sanitary pads and tampons
as luxuries
as if bleeding were indulgence
as if womanhood were a choice

while viagra and condoms
escaped taxation
as if male pleasure were essential
and female biology
was something to profit from

the gst has been lifted
but the disparities remain
toiletries
clothing
haircuts
personal services
costing more for women
because the system knows
women have been conditioned
to pay
to appease
to make do
to smooth over

a lifetime of paying more
for regularly used items
accumulates into harm
into financial instability
into futures compromised

and while women pay more
they earn less
the economic vise tightening
in both directions

women retire
with less superannuation
because super is tied to paid work
and unpaid work is invisible
unvalued
unaccounted for
women's caregiving
their domestic labour
their social glue
erased from the ledger
as though it were worth nothing

on average
women take home
about two hundred and forty dollars
less per week than men
twelve thousand dollars per year
a slow erosion
a constant draining
that compounds across decades

the pay gap is shaped
by recruitment discrimination
conscious bias
unconscious bias
undervaluation of female dominated industries

and the interruptions women face
from caregiving
from pregnancy
from illness
from ageing parents
from the demands of a society
that sees women as flexible labour
not full citizens

higher education is touted
as the great equaliser
but men are the primary beneficiaries
men graduate
step into higher paying jobs
repay their debts quickly
build wealth
advance careers

women graduate
step into lower paying industries
carry higher student debts for longer
face caregiving obligations
juggle labour that is unpaid
or underpaid
and repayment periods stretch
and stretch
and stretch
until financial stress
becomes permanent terrain

and then
there is the cost
of producing the next generation

women pay a disproportionate price
for continuing the species
having children is not a lifestyle choice
yet conservative leaders agonise
over declining fertility
over ageing populations
wringing hands about economic impact
while restricting abortion
restricting contraception
attempting to control women's bodies
to solve a problem
created by inequality

falling fertility rates in australia
are not a mystery
they are the natural consequence
of poverty
economic insecurity
unemployment
gender pay gaps
childcare that is inaccessible
or unaffordable
the cost of housing
the demands of caring for ageing parents
medical access
mental load
climate anxiety

making earning a living easier for women
makes it easier for them
to choose motherhood
if they wish
accessible childcare
affordable childcare
and paying childcare workers properly
investing in public education
these are essential
not optional

women provide the majority
of unpaid care and domestic labour
even when employed full time
workplace inflexibility
especially in senior roles
creates barriers to women's independence
their progression
their earning power

barriers to financial independence
create serious risks
for homelessness
particularly for single mothers
for women relying on part time wages
or parenting payments

domestic violence
dramatically increases homelessness risk
and is the most common reason
women present to australia's main
government homelessness program

to help women participate fully in the workplace
we must close the gender pay gap
value unpaid care
change societal norms
around domestic responsibility
and refuse to let another generation
of women age into poverty
or homelessness
because of a system
built to profit from their labour
while denying its worth
beneath these economic currents
mermaids swim
their tails heavy
with centuries of unpaid work
with generations of undervaluation
they carry the memory
of all the women who held families together
on wages that stretched too thin
on budgets carved from scarcity
they know
that the cost of being a woman
has never been accidental
it has been engineered
structured
maintained
but they also know
that tides change
and that nothing
not even the economy
is immune to rising waters

cultural misogyny

in these waters
cultural competence is a tide we must learn
a way of moving through currents
we did not create
a way of recognising
that the ocean holds many nations
many histories
many truths
and that first nations people
must learn to swim ethically
and effectively
in personal and professional waters
that were never theirs

cultural competence begins with reflection
with knowing one's own worldview
knowing the cultural lenses we wear
knowing how they bend the light
how they distort what we think we see
how they influence every choice
and how they determine
whether our presence is respectful
or harmful

it requires imagining across difference
collaborating across cultures
stepping gently where stories run deep
listening where silence is ceremony
knowing that respect is more than politeness
it is responsibility
reciprocity
relationship

because first nations people
should never have to fight harder to be believed
especially when women and girls go missing
their disappearances met with shrugs
with silence
with inaction
with the slow cruel tide
that shows which lives australia values
and which it does not

with a growing first nations population
with almost half of australians
born overseas or with migrant parentage
and with cultures layering over cultures
like shifting sands
we live in an increasingly diverse global
community
a mosaic
a tidepool
a living archive of stories
languages
rituals
and ways of knowing

cultural competence is about valuing diversity
not as an aesthetic
not as tokenism
but as a source of richness
creativity
innovation
truth
as something that strengthens society
rather than something society tolerates

at the national level
it requires real action
not statements
not slogans
not symbolic gestures
action to eradicate racism
action to embed truth telling
into classrooms
hospitals
media
parliament
services
into every system that shapes lives

it requires cultural safety
trauma informed training
in every sector
every service
so that first nations people
are not forced to translate their own pain
into palatable language
for institutions that caused the harm

and it requires
as a matter of urgency
investment into community based programs
not top down paternalism
but grassroots healing
led by first nations people
for first nations people
to address intergenerational trauma
to revive knowledge systems
law
languages
stories
songlines
to keep the ancient threads unbroken
to nourish futures
rooted in sovereignty

because social justice needs a voice
and that voice
is the uluru statement from the heart
a call offered with generosity
clarity
peace
and profound wisdom
a map toward a better continent
an invitation to walk together
not behind
not ahead
but with

beneath it all
mermaids swim
their tails shimmering with every culture
every memory
their voices carrying songs older than
colonisation
older than borders
songs reminding us
that no ocean is owned
that no land begins with arrival
that no nation thrives
when it silences its first storytellers

cultural misogyny diminishes everyone
but cultural competence
can raise the tide
for all

a rising that softens as it climbs
a tide that lifts us all before it settles
delivering calm waters
through the very act of rising
justice swelling into gentleness
the future arriving not as storm
but as a long slow breath
carrying every voice toward peace

digital misogyny

in the bright blue light
of phones
of laptops
of always on screens
a new ocean has formed
vast
borderless
without tide or moon
yet full of dangers
older than language

digital misogyny
is not separate from the world
it is the world
amplified
accelerated
unmasked

trolls swarm
like predatory fish
drawn to women's voices
women's achievements
women's joy
their goal
to harass
to frighten
to silence
to force retreat

incel culture grows
like poisonous algae
blooms of entitlement
choking the currents
men blaming women
for their loneliness
their resentment
their failures
turning rage into ideology
violence into belonging

porn conditioned violence
seeps through the network
rewiring boys
before they know
their own desires
teaching them
that women exist
for use
for harm
for domination
teaching them
that pain is normal
that consent is optional
that degradation is arousal
that humanity is disposable

deepfakes stalk women
stealing their faces
their bodies
their dignity
turning them into images
they never posed for
stories they never consented to
violence they never endured
yet must live with anyway
a violation
so new
the law still blinks
in confusion

stalking amplified by tech
tracking devices hidden
in handbags
cars
phones
apps designed for safety
repurposed for control
location shared
privacy shattered
women forced
to live smaller
to live quieter
to live under watch

and yet
beneath this digital ocean
another sea moves

mermaids swim
through fibre optic currents
their tails flickering
in pulses of light
their voices echoing
in the cables that lace
the ocean floor

they navigate
digital reefs
full of predators
who lurk behind avatars
and usernames
who strike from shadows
who hide their fear
beneath cruelty

mermaids know
this new ocean
is simply the old one
made visible
misogyny refracted
through code
through screens
through algorithms
designed by men
who never imagined
the harm
their biases could magnify

mermaids glide
through the data streams
carrying shields
made of truth
and community
and refusal

their presence
disrupts the circuitry
their voices
jam the frequencies
their resilience
rewrites the system
one shimmer at a time

and human women
do the same

they build networks
of resistance
block
report
document
expose
mourn
support
educate
refuse
return

even when the waters
are hostile
even when the predators
are many
even when the currents
drag them under

digital misogyny
tries to drown them
in notifications
in threats
in violence
coded and un-coded

but women rise
again and again
salt fierce
digital daughters
of mermaids
moving through
a world not designed
for their survival
yet surviving anyway

in the end
the predators
are predators
hiding in the shadows

but mermaids
women
queer folk
girls
survivors
swim in the open
lit by the glow
of their own endurance

and the digital ocean
trembles
knowing
they are learning
how to claim it

in the vast dark beneath the surface
where pressure builds
where light thins
where truth echoes louder
than any voice above
women with a disability move
with a strength unrecognised
unvalued
unprotected

disability and misogyny
collide like tectonic plates
creating a depth all their own
a trench carved
by centuries of exclusion
pity
dismissal
and exploitation

the world tells a women
with a disability
your worth is conditional
your autonomy negotiable
your needs inconvenient
your safety optional

carer violence
lurks in the quiet places
behind closed doors
in support services
in medical rooms
in homes where trust
is mandatory
yet rarely reciprocated

girls and women
with a disability
are taught
to be grateful
for basic care
for minimal access
for scraps of dignity
for tolerance
instead of belonging

gratefulness is weaponised
kindness used as currency
the threat always present
if you complain
you lose help
if you resist
you lose support
if you speak
you lose safety

women with a disability face
wage inequality
that stretches wider
than any ocean canyon
pushed into part time roles
low paid sectors
insecure work
or denied employment entirely
their labour seen as lesser
their capability doubted
their ambitions dismissed
before they can bloom

medical infantilisation
wraps around them
like a net
woven with patronising tones
slow speech
decisions made without them
choices taken from their hands
experts treating them
as perpetual children
as if disability erases adulthood
as if needing access
means lacking intellect
as if autonomy
is too heavy a burden
for them to hold

and beneath the waves
mermaids with scars
swim steadily
their tails shimmering
with stories no one asked to hear
but everyone expects them to hide

their bodies marked
not by weakness
but by survival
each scar a cartography
of battles fought
in worlds not built for them

yet they are told
again and again
that their beauty
their value
their desirability
their legitimacy
is conditional

conditional on health
conditional on compliance
conditional on gratitude
conditional on silence
conditional on how little
they demand

mermaids hear this from the surface
the constant message
be inspiring
but not complicated
be grateful
but not assertive
be brave
but never angry
be disabled
but not too disabled
do not disrupt
the narrative
that your suffering
must be pretty
palatable
productive

but mermaids with a disability
refuse these conditions
they rise with powerful strokes
through currents built against them
their scars catching the sunlight
their bodies sacred
not in spite of disability
but with it
through it
because of it

they remind the sea
and the land above
that independence
is not the only form
of strength
that interdependence
is a radical truth
that needing care
is not a flaw
that receiving help
should never mean
experiencing harm

women with a disability
deserve oceans
built around access
workplaces built around equity
medical systems built around respect
communities built around safety
relationships built around consent
and a world
in which their worth
is never again
conditional

beneath the waves
the mermaids gather
their scars glowing
their bodies unapologetic
their presence a rebellion
against every lie
they have ever been told

and together
they sing a song
strong enough
to split the seabed
a song that says
we deserve care
not exploitation
we deserve autonomy
not control
we deserve love
not tolerance
we deserve power
not pity
we deserve freedom
without conditions

disability and gendered care

in these waters
mermaids rise from riverbeds and tidal lakes
bodies shimmering
scales gleaming
movements shaped by currents
men will never feel
and still
the world judges them by land standards
standards carved by men
for men
with no room for tail or fin or difference

physical disability limits access
to venues built like fortresses
stairs like stone cliffs
doorways too narrow
corridors too tight
the ocean has no such barriers
but the land insists on them
as if to remind women
that the world
was never designed for their breath

in this culture
anger is policed
patrolled
caged

the anger allowed to people with a disability
must be small
must be quiet
must be directed inward
toward impairment
toward the body
toward the self
never outward
never toward the society
that refuses to remove the actual barriers
that disable us in the first place

when we turn our anger outward
as we should
as any mermaid fighting the current must
we are dismissed as bitter
too sharp
too emotional
too much

the social model of disability
is the current that finally speaks truth
it tells us clearly
that we are far more disabled
by hostile infrastructure
and indifferent attitudes
than we ever are by our bodies

that disability comes
not from being unable to use stairs
but from the presence of the stairs
from the refusal to build ramps
refusal to design inclusion
refusal to imagine a world
where everyone swims

men who care for a woman
with a disability
are praised
admired
pitied
cast as heroes for doing the bare minimum
their compassion inflated like sails
their sacrifices exaggerated into legend

but women
women are expected to be the natural carers
of family members with a disability
of elders
of children
of partners
of friends
their labour dissolved into the water
unseen
presumed
never acknowledged as extraordinary
only required

in the ocean
a mermaid supports another mermaid
and no one calls it noble
it is simply survival
but on land
the care work of women
is invisible currency
unpaid
unthanked
unending

and layered over this
gender inequity tears into the mind
sharp as coral
body image pressure
gendered demand
social judgement
these grind down women
feeding anxiety and depression
two to three times more prevalent
than in men
not because women are weak
but because the tide is heavier on their backs

fear of violence
fear of harassment
fear of what happens in dark streets
keeps women from public space
keeps them from walking home
keeps them from using transport

keeps them from belonging
in their own communities
turning the simple act of moving
through the world
into a gamble of safety

these are lives shaped
by abuse
fear
harassment
discrimination
by men who praise themselves
for caregiving
while women drown
beneath the expectation of it
by a society that designs its buildings
its services
its attitudes
to accommodate only the white
the able bodied
the male

yet even here
mermaids swim
fierce
unyielding
refusing to be made small
refusing to be tolerated
refusing to apologise
for taking up space
in oceans
in rivers
in streets
in clinics
in every place
a woman is meant to shrink

they rise
they carve channels through rigid systems
they drag whole worlds forward
with the strength of their tails

and the water remembers
every motion they make

economic misogyny

deep as a trench
relentless as a tide
threaded with the mermaids who know
what it means to have their labour
their existence
their value
rendered invisible

in this ocean of patriarchy
the economic system is a reef built crooked
a structure designed centuries ago
by men
for men
with biases cemented into its foundations
shaping every wave
every shore
every possibility

economic misogyny begins here
in the architecture
in the blueprints
in an economy that developed
with in built prejudice toward women
limiting their chances of success
long before
they ever walked into a workplace

a capitalist economy
fundamentally excludes women
devalues reproductive labour
erases caregiving
erases motherhood
erases emotional labour
while demanding all of it
for free

capitalism measures value
through profit
production
output
numbers
metrics
but it has no language
for feeding children
for holding elders
for tending the sick
for smoothing the world
keeping households alive
sustaining communities
healing harms
softening the human condition
these are not counted
and therefore
are not valued

this system
hostile to women
hostile to care
hostile to interdependence
becomes one of the core structures
that systematises misogyny
indoctrinates it
makes it invisible
makes it natural

economics is a predominantly male science
and the characteristics ascribed to men
are deemed more valuable
than those associated with women
logic valued over empathy
assertion valued over collaboration
competition valued
over cooperation
domination valued
over relational understanding

in this context
women are associated with emotional labour
and reproductive labour
the labour of care
the labour of life
the labour that sustains all other labour

and yet
there are no methods
to materially value this work
no frameworks
no accounting
no respect

the work that makes all work possible
is economically invisible
and so women
become even more disenfranchised
even more economically vulnerable
their subordination to male dominance
reinforced
by the very structure meant to support society

placing women in the informal sphere
is not an accident
it is maintenance
maintenance of male dominance
keeping women in the household
keeping them in low level roles
keeping them underpaid
keeping them precarious
keeping them dependent

traditional female jobs
are extensions of women's unpaid work
community service
nursing
childcare
admin
aged care
personal services
animal care
domestic work
event management
personal assistance
work shaped like servitude
work shaped like availability
work shaped to fit around men's careers
not women's lives

and so
a lifetime of unpaid and underpaid labour
leaves women facing later years
in poverty
in housing stress
in loneliness
with superannuation accounts empty
with wages that never caught up
with a future shaped
by the economic system
that always treated them
as afterthoughts

economic policies
are shaped by attitudes
stereotypes
expectations about women
their roles
their capabilities
their place
the belief that women's work is supplementary
that women's income is secondary
that women's ambitions must be flexible
that women's needs are negotiable

but mermaids rise in these waters
salt shimmering
tails scarred from centuries of undervaluation
their labour endless
their songs unheard

they know the truth
that care is the backbone of civilisation
that life continues
because of women's work
because of women's labour
because of women's unseen contributions

they swim through economies
built on their erasure
and whisper
you built all of this
on our backs
and called it natural

but the tide is shifting
the ocean remembers
and women
like mermaids surfacing
are reclaiming value
redefining labour
refusing erasure
refusing invisibility

economic misogyny
may be in the foundations
but so too
is women's power

and the sea
rises
with them

in this vast sea of misogyny
the waves break against everyone
against women first
but against men too
men taught that their worth is a performance
their identity a costume
their masculinity a brittle raft
that splinters the moment they reach
for something gentle
something green
something sustainable
men shun eco friendly choices
not from indifference
but from fear
fear of seeming soft
fear of being mocked
fear of being compared to women
as if femininity is contamination
as if care is corrosion
as if the planet itself is female
and therefore unworthy of respect

beneath these cultural tides
mermaids swim
watching men flounder
caught between desire and expectation

every muscle tense
every choice scrutinised
every environmental act interpreted
as a slip
a risk
a confession of femininity

men are exquisitely sensitive
to the trapdoors of gender
anything can mark them
a pink reusable bag
a colourful drink
a higher pitched laugh
a moment of grace
a piece of softness
their social survival always at stake

and meanwhile
plastic bags drift into oceans
nets and threads choke coral
microfibres tangle in seaweed
the waters thickening with shame
men choosing plastic
not because they want plastic
but because they fear
that a cloth bag
might cost them their place
in the hierarchy

mermaids weave through these currents
tails slicing through cloth scraps
nylon shreds
discarded synthetics
the debris of masculinity
made visible

this is the green feminine stereotype
a cultural spell that tells men
environmentalism is woman's work
cleaning up
recycling
mending
repairing
caring for the world
all considered feminine
all considered inferior
so men step back
and the ocean fills with consequence

and then there are the sailors
the old world mariners
the ones who believed every shoreline
was theirs to claim
every creature theirs to catch
every woman theirs to conquer
the myths of mermaids born from their fear
their longing
their violence
their hunger for domination
the same men who carved maps
as if earth were an object not a mother

and their modern heirs still roam the seas
fishermen turned industrial fleets
trawlers dragging massive nets
ripping the ocean floor bare
taking more than ecosystems can rebuild
stripping reefs
hauling life up in metallic fists
turning the living body of the sea
into profit
into product
into plunder

it is rape
of the ocean
of the future
of the mother who made us

mermaids watch from the deep
witnessing the nets scrape across their homes
reefs torn open
kelp forests uprooted
schools of fish vanished in minutes
centuries of balance lost in a single season
the ocean silenced
by engines
by greed
by the masculinity that believes
everything exists to be taken

and on land
advertising reinforces the script
powerful men
pretty women
macho cars
glossed over femininity
strength portrayed as consumption
dominance
speed
noise
and women reduced to adornment

the v8 supercar culture
celebrating the winner
with skimpily dressed women
draped like trophies
flowers and kisses handed out
as if femininity exists
to bless male triumph
as if power cannot be imagined
without patriarchy propping it up

this is the same narrative
that teaches men
environmentalism is emasculating
that caring is weak
that sustainability is soft
that the only real power
is combustion
extraction
violence

so when the prime minister
mocked electric vehicles in twenty nineteen
claiming they would ruin the weekend
scummo was defending not the economy
but the identity
the brittle masculinity
that fears any tool
not forged in smoke and fire

this was the same man
who held up a lump of coal
in parliament
like a trophy
mocking renewables
mocking battery storage
mocking the future
clinging to the past
as though patriarchy itself
were a resource that could never run out

but the ocean knows better
the mermaids know better
the reefs know better
the tide knows better

masculinity must soften
expand
heal
release its grip on domination

for the earth cannot survive
under a system that treats care as shame
that treats protection as weakness
that treats the ocean
as a woman to be conquered

in these waters
mermaids rise
salt shimmering
eyes ancient
tails radiant with the memory
of every vanished species
every polluted tide
every broken reef

they call men back to themselves
not the narrow selves
the world forced on them
but the full selves
capable of love
capable of care
capable of protecting
rather than plundering

because the sea of misogyny
harms everyone
men included
and healing the earth
requires healing masculinity
healing culture
healing the stories we tell
about strength

for the ocean belongs to no one
and everyone
and she is calling
for a different kind of manhood
one that rises like the tide
into partnership with the earth
not ownership of her

environmental misogyny

every culture
has its version of the earth goddess
the greeks called her gaia
others named her differently
some names lost
some whispered in dust
some carried only in songs
older than language
older than writing
older than the rise of the first stone walls

in every corner of the globe
shrines were built to her
statues carved
paintings left in caves
as if humanity knew from the beginning
that the earth was not an object
but a mother
a body
a presence
a goddess holding them alive

gaia inhabited the planet
offering life
offering nourishment
offering breath
in ancient civilisations she was revered
mother
nurturer
giver of life

the one who forms land from chaos
the one who shapes order from primordial dark
the one who gives structure to the formless
the first power
the oldest pulse
the original law

to the greeks she was raw maternal force
the ultimate goddess
the spirit arriving
when everything awaited direction
when the earth
was still dreaming itself into being
she gave bones to the sky
skin to the mountains
blood to the rivers
and the world unfolded beneath her hands

but history is kept by the victors
and the victors are most often men
so gaia was diminished
relegated to mythology
told her throne was imagination
not truth
her power rewritten
her authority belittled
her divinity dismissed

this is environmental misogyny
the internalised contempt for mother earth
for the feminine divine
for the idea that the planet is alive
intelligent
self regulating
capable of autonomy

yet even science eventually remembered
what the old stories knew

in the nineteen seventies
lynn margulis and james lovelock
proposed a heresy
that the earth is a living being
self regulating its systems to sustain life
their gaia hypothesis
mocked
argued
dismissed
slowly rose into acceptance
until the scientific world finally admitted
that the earth behaves as a unified organism
that chemicals speak to one another
that oceans and atmospheres converse
that forests pulse
that geology breathes
that life stabilises itself through endless
communication
a sophisticated intelligence
woven through soil water fire air

the early theory
that a conscious universe regulates the planet
no longer sounds impossible
only ancient
only long known
only ignored

yet modern culture continues to treat gaia
as something to exploit
to extract
to burn
to bury
to consume

we use single use materials
soft plastics
synthetics
petrochemical throwaways
as if the earth were a bottomless pit
but there is no away
gaia is a fishbowl
a closed system
nothing leaves
everything remains
plastic becomes dust
dust becomes ocean
ocean becomes blood

slowly
australian culture is shifting
away from the linear economy
of bash burn and bury
the old violent logic
that assumes resources are unlimited
that the planet will always recover
that mother earth can endure endless blows
because she is mother
because she is woman
because misogyny teaches us
that women will cope
will stretch
will survive
no matter what we take

but we are learning
there is another way
a circular economy
an economy aligned with gaia's cycles
one that eliminates waste
circulates materials
regenerates nature
one that mirrors the ocean
the forest
the shifting seasons
the recycling of all things

the circular economy gives us tools
to tackle climate change
to confront biodiversity loss
to meet social needs
without consuming the earth
it gives us power
to grow resilience
to grow prosperity
to grow jobs
while cutting emissions
waste
pollution

the linear model
take make discard
is a wound
a slow self poisoning

in a circular model
we stop producing waste at its source
we design with return in mind
we treat matter as sacred
nothing disposable
nothing beneath value

three principles guide this tide
eliminate waste and pollution
circulate products and materials
at their highest value
regenerate nature

all underpinned by renewable energy
renewable materials
renewable mindsets

a circular economy separates economic activity
from the consumption of finite resources
it builds a resilient system
good for business
good for people
good for the environment
good for gaia herself

and in these waters
mermaids rise
ocean goddesses
salt daughters
heralds of a new tide
their voices urging us
to return to reciprocity
to honour mother earth
to honour ourselves

for the planet is alive
and she remembers
every choice
every wound
every act of care
she still offers us the chance
to choose differently
to choose life
to choose regeneration
to choose reverence
before the tide runs out

everyday misogyny

in the wide salt world
misogyny is not only the storms
not only the headlines
not only the bruises and the breaking
it is also the daily drip
the constant erosion
the thousand small cuts
that shape a woman's life

beyond the workplace
it floats everywhere
in cafes
in supermarkets
in streets
in family gatherings
in waiting rooms
in the casual spaces
where danger hides in politeness

interruptions
the first tide
the most ordinary
the assumption
that a woman's voice is background noise
a soft soundtrack
that can be faded out
or spoken over
or swallowed
before it forms meaning

mansplaining
the second tide
a man explaining
your own knowledge back to you
as though you are a sponge
not a thinker
as though every woman is a student
and every man is a teacher
as though your years
your expertise
your lived experience
have the weight of sea foam

street harassment
the third tide
the hot breath at a bus stop
the car window sliding down
the whispered comment
the shout across the street
the glance that lingers too long
the leer disguised as compliment
the men who call it harmless
the women who know it is not

and beneath all this
the constant recalibration of safety
every woman
every girl
running calculations silently
doors locked
keys between fingers
phone charged
eyes scanning for exits
the instinctive loop
of assessing
predicting
surviving

mermaids rise here too
navigating the surface world
where threat glints like broken shells
where danger arrives wrapped in politeness
where men say relax
i am just being friendly
and women feel the undertow
pulling at their ankles

mermaids who know
that a smile is armour
that eye contact is negotiation
that a firm no is often a provocation
that softness can be mistaken for invitation
that safety is built
moment by moment
choice by careful choice

the microaggressions whirl together
a storm in slow motion
the man who stands too close in a queue
the uncle who comments on your body
the stranger who touches your back
to move you aside
the friend who jokes that you're too sensitive
the boss who says you'd be prettier
if you smiled

these daily abrasions
wear grooves in the soul
each one small
each one survivable
each one explainable
yet together
an ocean

and women learn young
to navigate these waters
to read the shift in tone
the tilt of a head
the tightening of a jaw
the darkening of a street
to measure whether they can walk
or should run

mermaids swim between worlds
the deep
where truth is spoken
and the surface
where danger pretends to be benign
they know
that misogyny does not always roar
sometimes it whispers
sometimes it smiles
sometimes it apologises
sometimes it waits

but they also know
that naming the tide
changes its pull
that visibility
is the first step toward safety
that truth turned into voice
is a form of armour

and so the story telling
lays bare the quiet violences
the subtle hurts
the tiny rips in the fabric of a woman's day

because the thousand small cuts
are not small at all
they are the tides
women swim against
every single day

financial abuse and economic control

in the spectrum of violence
some wounds leave no bruises
no fingerprints
no police photographs
only empty bank accounts
restricted access
vanished pay
and futures stolen quietly
line by line

financial abuse
is a form of domestic violence
as sharp
as any blade
as suffocating
as any locked door

it begins slowly
withheld bank cards
monitored spending
questions that masquerade
as concern
then become interrogation
then become command

wages are extracted
before they reach a woman's hands
deposited into joint accounts
she cannot access
or accounts she does not even know exist
her labour taken
her earnings absorbed
her autonomy drained
into someone else's pockets

women are trapped
through debt
debts created without their consent
credit cards opened in their names
loans approved with forged signatures
bills hidden
payments missed deliberately
until the numbers grow monstrous

women are trapped
through dependence
told they are bad at money
told they can't be trusted
told they don't understand
told they should be grateful
for being provided for
while every dollar becomes
another chain
another shackle
another proof
that escape is impossible

economic abuse is cunning
it renders leaving dangerous
staying necessary
it strips away options
until a woman believes
there are none

beneath the waves
mermaids struggle too
tangled not in rope
but in nets woven from money
from withheld resources
from economic control

their tails thrash
against invisible constraints
currents that pin them
currents that whisper
you cannot survive alone
currents built from scarcity
manufactured by another's greed

mermaids feel the drag
as bank accounts are seized
as earnings are rerouted
as treasures they collected
are confiscated
as their mobility narrows
their world shrinks
their ability to surface
diminishes

underwater
currency glitters differently
shells
pearls
precious metals
but the harm feels the same
someone hoarding the resources
someone controlling access
someone deciding
what she is allowed to hold
to own
to earn
to dream

economic nets
are some of the strongest
because they are unseen
because they are legal
because they are silent
because they can be framed
as love
as care
as protection

but mermaids
slowly
surely
learn to cut through
these nets

with community
with knowledge
with whispered warnings
with shared strategies
with the fierce truth
that money is not love
that control is not care
that dependence is not devotion

they rise
carrying women with them
toward a world
where bank accounts
are private
debt is not weaponised
earnings are not extracted
and autonomy
is never surrendered
for security

a world
where financial safety
is a right
not a gift
where economic independence
is the floor
not the ceiling
where leaving
is possible
because money
is no longer
a cage

beneath the waves
the mermaids gather
in circles of solidarity
cutting the nets
thread by thread
until all that remains
is water
and freedom

and woven through all of this
is the truth we whisper quietly
because saying it aloud stings
women see the climate collapsing
before many men will even glance
at the horizon
women feel the shift of drought
the panic of empty shelves
the sickness of smoke
the weight of rising heat
deep in their bodies
in their gardens
in the small domestic ecosystems they tend
the ones men often never notice

women watch the climate unravel
because they carry the load
they carry the household
the food the water the children
they feel each change as rupture
as threat
as responsibility
as something that must be faced now

while many men
especially those shielded by power
those high in right wing political parties
still lift the economy like a shield
saying not yet
not now
too expensive
too inconvenient
too disruptive
to the industries that hold them up

they call concern hysteria
alarmism
emotional exaggeration
as though rising seas care about male egos
as though collapsing ecosystems will pause
to check if the quarterly figures are stable

some men treat the economy
as if it is the only earth worth saving
as if profit margins outrank coral reefs
as if jobs in dying industries
matter more than species extinction
as if mining expansions
and more coal
matter more than children breathing clean air
as if climate denial
is a mark of strength
rather than fear

women keep speaking
women keep marching
women keep organising
because they know
that climate change collapses silently
until it collapses loudly
and by then it is too late

they know the economy is a human invention
but the climate is a natural law
the earth will not negotiate
with market forces
the sea will not bargain
with political donors

and still
in parliament
in press conferences
in party rooms filled with men in dark suits
the refrain echoes
what about the economy
what about jobs
what about growth

while outside those walls
women pick up the pieces
women plant gardens in dry soil
women push strollers through bushfire smoke
women ration food when crops fail
women bury wildlife
found dying in their driveways

women hold communities together
when disasters hit again and again

this gendered divide
is not softness versus strength
but vision versus denial
stewardship versus self preservation
future versus fear

and in this story telling
the tide turns slowly
because women have always been the ones
to feel the earth's pulse
to listen to the soil
to notice the changes in the wind

and the question rises again
like a warning buoy in rough water
how long can a nation survive
when half of it sees the fire
and the other half insists the smoke
is simply steam from a thriving economy

gender based violence

in these waters
every week in australia
a woman is drowned
by the hands of a man she knows
current or former partner
the tides of intimacy turned lethal
her life taken
her name lost to headlines
her story swallowed by a culture
that keeps repeating
he was a great bloke
we did not see it coming
we did not hear the warnings
we did not want to look

violence against women is a leading cause
of illness
disability
premature death
not a side issue
not a distraction
not a private matter
the leading cause
the most predictable storm
in the nation's weather

and the waters run murkier still
for women with disabilities
for culturally diverse women
for first nations women
who are thirty two times more likely
to be admitted to hospital for domestic violence
thirty two times
as if their lives are worth less
as if this nation is willing
to sacrifice them to the waves

but violence is preventable
the tide is not natural
it is shaped by gender norms
by rigid stereotypes
masculinity as dominance
femininity as submission
the ancient script of patriarchy
still taught like gospel
still performed like ritual
still enforced like law

the drivers rise like rips in the ocean
condoning violence against women
normalising disrespect
aggressive male peer groups
limitations on women's independence
the boys club disguised as culture
as tradition
as harmless fun
while women drown quietly beneath it

over and over
women and girls report the same stories
the same waves hitting them
insults
denigration
humiliation
unwanted touching
groping
patronising dismissal
trolling
objectification
online and off
threats and harassment
judgement of looks
scrutiny of desirability
men treating women's bodies
as public property
as open territory
as coastlines to be claimed

these experiences accumulate
layer upon layer
like sediment thickening the seabed
creating a climate of fear
barriers invisible but immovable
limiting what women can do
where they can go
how they can exist

there is hardly a woman
who does not self safe guard
risk assessing from childhood
girls trained not in confidence
but in caution
walk with keys in your hand
don't wear this
don't go there
don't be alone
don't drink too much
don't trust too easily
don't provoke
don't relax
don't breathe free

if something happens
it will be your fault
the lesson sunk deep
the lesson carried for life

how many men
after a night at the pub
turn to their mates and say
text me when you get home safe
almost none
but women do it always
because danger is a tide that follows us
from bus stops to car parks
from workplaces to bedrooms
from daylight to dark

boys are not schooled
in how to avoid putting girls in fear
they are schooled in winning
in conquering
in owning
in entitlement
in taking rejection as insult
not information
and so many men
turn hostile when ignored
turn vicious when refused
turn dangerous
when a woman simply says *no*

public transport becomes treacherous
a compliment becomes a threat
a chat becomes a hunt
women scanning for passers by
for escape routes
for a witness
for anything that will keep them alive

stalking is its own tide
unwanted repeated contact
that tightens like a net
following
waiting
giving gifts
appearing at workplaces
lurking near homes
threatening harm

coercive control disguised as concern
predators acting when no one else is watching
violating boundaries
privacy
dignity
and leaving women isolated
frightened
exhausted

and in the workplace
victims fade
productivity crumbles
concentration shatters
absences accumulate
fear keeps them home
legal battles drain them
trauma bleeds into every part of life

until they have no choice but to quit
leaving income
leaving stability
leaving dreams
because one man decided her freedom
was his to take

women almost never lie about abuse
statistically
it is extremely unlikely
yet they are disbelieved
dismissed
undermined
smeared
failed by a system
that prioritises male freedom
over female survival

women leave their homes
their communities
their jobs
to escape violent men
their financial futures ruptured
while the nation shrugs
as if this devastation is collateral
as if male violence is weather
not choice

men continue to kill women
and australia continues
to offer condolences
instead of solutions
thoughts and prayers
instead of action
safety plans
instead of safety itself

we must create spaces
to engage men in this conversation
invite men to transform
challenge each other
be upstanders not bystanders
say something
speak against abuse
confront sexism
call out misogyny

challenge male stereotypes
grow healthier masculinities
shed entitlement like dead skin

talk about mental health
refuse the lie
that vulnerability is weakness
offer empathy
support
care

take accountability
teach boys differently
teach men differently
reshape culture from the inside

and above all
listen to women
believe women
their disclosures are lifelines
their truth a compass
their survival a map

violence will not end
until men become part of the solution
until men recognise their privilege
their safety
their power
until men see
how uneven the ocean truly is

if you are a man in australia
you are statistically safer
richer
more represented in leadership
less likely to face violence or discrimination
if you are white and able bodied
you float even higher
if you are straight
you will not face the dangers
that LGBTQIA+ people do

the waters are not equal
have never been equal
women swim against currents
that men create
that men maintain
that men must dismantle

and still
women rise
mermaids with storm winds in their hair
teeth bared
tails strong
fierce as tidal waves
demanding a world
where safety is not a luxury
where freedom is not a risk
where their lives
are not swallowed
by the deep

misogyny does not begin in adulthood
it arrives early
quiet as a ripple
sharp as a fin
shaping girlhood before girls
understand its name

in childhood
girls learn the rules
the unspoken ones
the ones carved beneath skin
the ones whispered in warnings
the ones woven into bedtime stories
the ones that tell them
be small
be careful
be quiet
be good

dress codes come first
hems tugged down
shoulders covered
knees policed
girls told their bodies are distractions
their skin a hazard
their limbs a problem
that must be managed
contained
hidden

sexualisation follows close behind
the adult gaze pressed onto young flesh
the murmured comments
the too long stares
the questions
the judgments
the sudden shift
from child
to object
from free
to watchful
from wild
to wary

silencing arrives soon after
don't make a fuss
don't be dramatic
don't argue
don't talk back
don't be rude
don't be bossy
don't be too loud
don't be too smart
don't be too proud
don't take up the space
saved for boys

girls learn quickly
that their freedom is conditional
that their bodies are monitored
that their safety is fragile
that their voices are negotiable

the abrupt shrinking of freedom
a tide pulling away
girls once roaming streets
now told to stay close
girls once climbing trees
now told to sit properly
girls once running barefoot
now told to be careful
be cautious
be aware
be afraid

girlhood becomes
a rehearsal for womanhood
a slow training
in vigilance
in self protection
in anticipating danger
in quiet survival

and beneath the waves
mermaid adolescents rise
young
strong
still bright with possibility
learning too soon
that even the sea is not safe

that sailors watch
that predators swim close
that currents can turn
that freedom is policed
underwater as much as on land

mermaid girls feel the shift
feel the safety slip
feel the water thicken
with danger
with expectation
with the weight
of becoming female

they are warned
don't swim alone
don't explore too far
don't trust too easily
don't shine too brightly
someone will notice
someone will want
someone will take

mermaid adolescents learn
the underwater version
of dress codes
don't let your tail shimmer too much
don't let your hair float too freely
don't let your voice echo too loudly
beauty becomes risk
and hiding becomes habit

they learn
that their bodies
are both power
and liability
that their voices
can summon peace
or provoke threat
that their freedom
is conditional
on the behaviour of others

girlhood shrinks
like a tide pulled back
leaving them standing
on exposed reef
barefoot
unprepared
told to grow up
but not too much
told to stay safe
but without tools
told to be good
but never bold

and yet
girls
human and mermaid
are fierce
even in this shrinking
they push back
they question
they resist
they dream
they swim toward deeper waters
even when warned
they carry an ancient strength
that misogyny cannot drown

girlhood may be shaped
by the loss of safety
but it is also shaped
by courage
by the first sparks of rebellion
by the understanding
that freedom is worth fighting for

and mermaid adolescents
learn early
that the sea
like the land
can be changed

judicial misogyny

in this patriarchal ecosystem
misogyny grows like deep sea rust
embedded in every beam of the judicial
structure
a combination of misogynistic and racist
currents
particularly toxic
cutting through courts
police stations
law chambers
as natural as breathing
as devastating as a storm surge

there is a rising tide of anger
a swell of refusal
over the inability
the unwillingness
of the criminal justice system
to address the violence abuse degradation
that saturates women's and girls' daily lives
debates about this failure now centre stage
but they rise in a climate of polarisation
where vicious conduct spills unchecked
turbo charged by online disinhibition
anonymity
social media invasiveness
the digital ocean

in recent years
more and more women have broken their
enforced silence
spoken of domestic abuse
spoken of rape
spoken of sexual violence
spoken of the law's inadequacy
spoken of lives blighted
spoken of the impossibility
of achieving justice
and in speaking
they cracked the surface
until politicians had no choice
but to hear the roar beneath

not all men are abusive
but all women have experienced abusive
behaviour from men
and good decent men
are finally stepping forward
wanting to examine root causes
wanting to eradicate the mindset
that makes violence possible
these men desire change
and change demands they come

significant efforts have been made
to reform the law concerning rape
sexual offences
domestic abuse
yet some behaviours are so normalised
so trivialised
that law enforcement officials fail to act
misogynistic acts
threats
harassment
verbal attacks
the daily round of insult
still dismissed as too small
too everyday
too womanly
to matter

but these so called low level harms
are the foundation of the ocean women drown in
the daily grind of sexism harassment abuse
degrades women's lives
and the criminal justice system
fails to understand the ramifications
of this constant erosion
this constant abrasion

and girls
watching from childhood
learn their subordinate status
learn to shrink their voices
learn to doubt their confidence
learn to ask less
demand less
expect less

wider cultural change requires legislation
education
public awareness
a suite of solutions
not a single patch

and the harm compounds
for women who belong to minorities
women of colour
first nations women
migrant women
trans women
older women
queer women
women with a disability
religious minorities
each facing multiple levels of hostility
racist misogyny
religious misogyny
bias
police dismissal
invisibility

first nations women
are twenty one times more likely
to be imprisoned in australia
than non indigenous women
a statistic that reveals
what community policing really values
what it protects
and who it targets

misogyny is so deeply embedded
that measuring it becomes nearly impossible
a man may hate
women who challenge the status quo
or women who proudly display sexuality
or women who are opinionated
too powerful
too successful
too clever
too beautiful
not beautiful enough
too independent
too anything but submissive

the law claims neutrality
claims gender does not matter
claims it cannot favour one sex
but neutrality is a mask
that disguises male default
the presumption that male experience
is universal
and female suffering
is peripheral

rape is where the legal system collapses entirely
where misogyny permeates policing
prosecuting
trial systems
where myths and stereotypes about women
inform every decision
rape seen as lust
instead of violence
rape by a stranger privileged
above rape by a partner
as if knowing your attacker
lessens the violation

women are humiliated in cross examination
their credibility shredded
their trauma weaponised against them
their bodies scrutinised
their lives dissected
while the defendant remains silent
protected
unquestioned
untouched

lawyers deploy sexism
deploy misogyny
deploy bullying tactics
to intimidate demean ridicule survivors
going to court becomes the second rape
reliving the violence
the terror
the shame
the screaming silence

and on social media
vilification multiplies
an amplified version
of the revictimisation women face
for speaking
for reporting
for surviving
a pressure so intense
it silences countless women
before they can even begin

women's lives are torn apart
their families and friends
dragged into witness boxes
while the accused says nothing
offers nothing
faces nothing
this is australia's national shame
the plaintiff scrutinised
the accused protected
justice inverted

rape survivors who speak
are punished again
shamed
disbelieved
criticised
dismissed by support providers
by friends
by police
by courts
negative reactions that sew their mouths shut
until silence feels safer
than truth

most men who sexually assault women
are not monsters in the dark
they are out in the open
friends
colleagues
relatives
strangers in bright daylight
neighbours
community members
ordinary men
this is the truth we fear
there are no monsters in the sea
there are only people
just us

and like the original little mermaid
the myth before disney softened her
women walk the lonely road
with the sensation of metal blades
piercing their feet
every step agony
every step silenced
every step voiceless

women who have survived male violence
watch their abusers live celebrated lives
promoted
praised
protected
in positions of power
in positions of influence
their privilege intact
their reputations whole
while survivors
carry the trauma
the shame
the loneliness

the message is clear
to victims
to all women
you are worth less
than the men who harmed you
your pain
is inconvenience
your humanity
is negotiable

despite reforms
women do not get justice
and they know it
their trust in policing
and legal processes
is low
earned by experience
earned by failure
earned by silence

but #metoo
historic child sex abuse revelations
the toxic churn of online spaces
the omnipresence of porn
have increased the volume
women once forced to whisper
now roar
women once drowned
now rise

mermaids drag themselves from the surf
bleeding from knife sharp stones
tails heavy with salt
voices hoarse
but rising
rising
refusing to be silent any longer

the law may be a male oriented ocean
but women
are the tide
and the tide
always returns

medical misogyny

in these waters
women swim with currents against them
mermaids navigating reefs built from doubt
kelp forests tangled with disbelief
their bodies carrying stories
that doctors taught to listen only to men
often refuse to hear

there are unique challenges
shadows beneath the surface
that pull at women and girls
delayed diagnosis
pain dismissed
symptoms treated as exaggeration
or imagination
or inconvenience

in the male dominated medical system
the care offered for menstruation
for reproductive health
for menopause
for consent
for pain
rests on a misogynist foundation
the bedrock built by men
for men
shaped by centuries of deciding
that women's suffering
is simply the nature of the tide

a young girl shows signs of adhd
she swims in circles
loses focus in choppy waters
holds tension deep beneath her skin
yet no one sees her
they say she is dreamy
emotional
sensitive
they do not see the storm inside her
because they are taught to look
only for the boy version
of the same cyclone
so she goes undiagnosed
for years
until she has swallowed enough shame
to fill an ocean trench
another woman speaks of crippling pelvic pain
waves that bend her in half
storms that steal her breath
doctors tell her to relax
to take painkillers
to calm down
to wait it out
they call it normal
they call it stress
they call it anything except true
until at last
after years of drowning in agony
the truth surfaces

severe endometriosis
roots woven deep
damage long ignored

the medical world treats heart disease
differently in women
cancer differently
autism differently
basing its knowledge on male data
male symptoms
male bodies
then generalising outward
as if women are simply smaller men
as if physiology bends to patriarchy

medical misogyny rises from three tides
social prejudice
medical ignorance
research exclusion
the old belief that if it is not studied in men
it cannot be known
and so women's bodies remain
half mapped oceans
uncharted coastlines
misunderstood currents

intersectionality deepens the wound
racism meets misogyny
in the bodies of aboriginal and torres strait
islander women
who experience higher burdens of disease
higher barriers to care
higher risk at every turn

reproductive justice cannot exist
without racial equity
without economic equity
without cultural safety held like warm current
through every clinic every hospital every system

ending obstetric violence
addressing institutional racism
transforming cultural determinants of health
ensuring cultural safety is not an afterthought
these should be priorities
but too often they drift at the edges
like unanchored boats

girls avoid exercise
in early adolescence
waves of social pressure
pushing them back to shore
body image tightening around them like nets
confidence slipping away
until movement
joyful movement
becomes something to fear
something to hide

women are less physically active
at every age
the ocean narrows around them
their time swallowed by care
their confidence confiscated

their presence in gyms and sports clubs
met with judgement
with scrutiny
with the silent tightening of space
nearly half of women over twenty five
feel out of place in those rooms
forty per cent feel embarrassed
to exercise in public
as if their bodies are intruders
unwelcome swimmers in a male dominated sea

in this story telling
women are mermaids forced to swim upstream
against tides designed by men
their pain unnamed
their health not prioritised
their stories unheard

and still
they keep swimming
carving paths through hostile waters
learning to rewrite the maps
that never included them

in this wide heaving world
women carry the weather
of everyone around them
expected to soothe
smooth
mediate
heal
absorb
to be the balm
the bridge
the buffer
the steadying hand
the safe harbour
women are taught early
that their emotions must be tidy
their anger discreet
their grief folded small
their needs second
or third
or last

their mental health
treated like an inconvenience
a side note
a weakness
a private matter
to be managed quietly
with a smile
with a soft tone
with a whispered apology
for taking up space

they are the ones who calm the room
cool tempers
translate silences
read danger
sense tension
carry the emotional load
like invisible armour

they are mediators
between siblings
between parents
between co workers
between partners
between friends
between worlds

they are the ones
who remember birthdays
send messages
write cards
bring casseroles
show up
reach out
soften blows
patch wounds
pick up pieces

while inside
their own storms are gathering

women who soothe
often have no one
to soothe them
women who heal
often have nowhere
to lay their own brokenness
women who absorb
carry the weight of others
without anyone
to help carry theirs

burnout hides in their bones
an exhaustion that feels tidal
mental health eroding
in unseen ways
because society rewards
their selflessness
while demanding more
and more
and more

enter the mermaids
keepers of the emotional tides
feeling every shift
every pressure
every pull
from the surface world

mermaids are expected
to hold whole communities
their songs used
to settle storms
their presence used
to ease the heavy waters
their empathy taken
as naturally as breath

they sense grief
travel through currents
heavy with unspoken sorrow
they listen to the heartbeats
of the broken
they carry strangers' secrets
in the silence between waves

yet when their own hearts crack
the sea rarely listens
rarely holds them
rarely soothes the ones
who soothe everyone else

mermaids know
the dangerous myth
of the strong woman
the one who never wavers
never falls
never asks
never breaks
never needs

they know how this myth
is used to justify neglect
how emotional labour becomes
an expectation
a duty
a quiet unpaid tax

and they whisper
beneath the waves
that strength
is not endurance
strength is not silence
strength is not swallowing pain

true strength
is asking to be held
refusing to drown quietly
allowing softness
claiming rest
claiming help
claiming the right
to unravel

the emotional labour women carry
is vast
ancient
passed down
through generations
like an heirloom
and an anchor

yet the tide is shifting
as women name the weight
as mermaids refuse to carry
entire oceans alone
as mental health becomes
not shame
but sanctuary

one day
women will not be expected
to hold everyone together
while falling apart themselves
one day
the emotional currents
will be shared
evenly
respectfully
humanly

and on that day
mermaids will rise
unburdened
singing their own healing
not just the healing of others

migration and misogyny

migration
is never just movement
it is rupture
exile
reinvention
a shedding
and a searching

and for migrant women
refugee women
climate displaced women
the journey is lined
with misogyny
woven into borders
papers
systems
languages
laws

visa vulnerability
is its own kind
of violence
women tied
to partners
to employers
to sponsors
to strangers
their safety held
by the thin thread
of documentation

one threat
from a husband
one complaint
from a boss
one withheld form
can unravel
their entire world

abuse flourishes
in this vulnerability
because perpetrators know
that women
cannot leave
cannot report
cannot defend
cannot risk deportation
cannot risk separation
from their children
cannot risk losing
the little stability
they have managed
to build

migrant women exploited
in workplaces
harvest fields
factories
cleaning jobs
hospitality
care work
their labour underpaid
their visas used
as leverage
their bodies endangered
their boundaries ignored

refugees from wars
fleeing bombed cities
mass graves
occupied homelands
lose not only place
but identity
profession
extended family
records
history
status

they carry trauma
grief
survival
and still
are met
by suspicion
surveillance
racism
xenophobia
and the quiet violence
of being unwanted

climate refugees
a growing tide
women forced from lands
that have fed their ancestors
from rivers gone dry
from soil gone to dust
from storm shattered homes
from sinking islands

their displacement
is not recognised
as legitimate
by nations
that caused
the climate crisis
yet refuse
to open borders
to those drowning
in its aftermath

cultural policing
follows them
across oceans
across borders
across generations

women told
they are too westernised
or not western enough
too free
or insufficiently free
too visible
or not visible enough
too modern
or too traditional
every choice
critiqued
controlled
condemned

the loss of community
cuts deepest
when language
places
familiar foods
familiar seasons
familiar songs
familiar storytellers
are gone

women rebuild
from memory
constructing identity
from fragments
from recipes
from lullabies
from whatever survived
the crossing

and beneath the waves
mermaids uprooted
know this story well

mermaids forced
from coral homes
by warming oceans
bleaching reefs
industrial trawlers
deep sea mining
polluted currents

they swim
into new waters
where nothing
tastes the same
where the sand
feels unfamiliar
where the creatures
do not welcome them

they are strangers
in oceans
they once thought
were endless

mermaids trying
to adapt
to new ecosystems
with old scars
with old stories
with old songs
that do not echo right
in foreign currents

some currents
push them back
some predators
circulate lies
some reefs
close their doors

migration
is a kind of grief
even in the sea

and human women
mirror this pain

migrant mermaids
and migrant women
share the same
lonely courage
the same tenacity
the same refusal
to disappear

they carry
their mother tongues
in their mouths
their memories
in their bones
their culture
in the way they cook
their hope
in the way they keep going

and though the new oceans
may not welcome them
they still swim
still strive
still rebuild

migrant women
are the architects
of new worlds
even when the old ones
are lost

they teach us
that home
is not always a place
sometimes
it is a refusal
sometimes
it is a survival
sometimes
it is a future
built from nothing
but will

mermaids rise
to meet them
in solidarity
salt to salt
song to song

whispering
you belong
even when the world
pretends
you don't

misogyny does not only live
in laws
in offices
in public spaces
it lives also
in the quiet rooms
between women
woven into friendship
braided into childhood
passed down
like an inheritance
no one asked for

women are pressured
into competition
from the first day
they are compared
ranked
measured
against one another

who is prettier
who is thinner
who is nicer
who is more desirable
who is more disciplined
who is more agreeable
who fits what men want

friendship becomes
a strange choreography
of closeness and caution
care and comparison
love and fear

girls learn early
to distrust one another
learn that only a few
can be chosen
can be liked
can be praised
and that every girl
must fight quietly
for her place

this pressure
is not accidental
it is engineered
it is the architecture
of patriarchy
the divide and conquer
of female solidarity

internalised misogyny
seeps in slowly
teaching women
to judge each other
before men can
to shame each other
before society does
to see rivals
instead of allies
to believe
that another woman's rise
is their own fall

mean girl stereotypes
are built on this
cartoon villain versions
of girls and women
created to obscure
the real source of harm
created to make us believe
that girls hurt girls
because girls are cruel
when the truth
is girls hurt girls
because society trains them to
because men's approval
becomes the currency
they are forced to trade
because scarcity
is manufactured
to keep women divided

and the policing
of female solidarity
is relentless

women who defend each other
are called cliques
women who uplift each other
are mocked
women who trust each other
are suspicious
women who form powerful circles
are ridiculed
dismissed
weakened with jokes
about cattiness
jealousy
pettiness
insecurities

because patriarchy knows
that if women ever unite
deeply
fully
ferociously
everything changes

beneath the waves
mermaid pods learn
this truth early

they are born
into currents
designed to separate them
whirlpools of scarcity
tides of competition
shoals of predators
who benefit
when mermaids
swim alone

but mermaid pods
learn to trust each other
in the dark water
in the bright shallows
in the coral forests
where secrets
and dangers
and memories
are shared

they learn
that survival
is communal
that strength
is collective
that power
multiplies
when women
swim together

mermaids braid their hair
with sea grass
and shared stories
they form circles
to protect their young
they warn each other
of sharks
and shipwrecks
and sailors
with nets disguised
as kindness

they rise together
hunt together
heal together
refuse isolation
refuse competition
refuse the myths
written about them

they know
what human women
are remembering now

solidarity
is the deepest magic
connection
is the fiercest rebellion
trust
is the strongest current
women can build

in the end
misogyny in friendship
is not natural
it is constructed

and mermaids
like women
are tearing down
the architecture
brick by brick
wave by wave

until friendship
becomes sanctuary
again

misogyny does not always roar
sometimes it whispers
inside kitchens
hallways
childhood bedrooms
family gatherings
where the first lessons
of gender
are carved into bone

daughters raised differently than sons
before they understand why
before language
before memory

daughters taught
to be careful
to be helpful
to be quiet
to be kind
to be small
to be grateful
to be pretty
to be patient
to be forgiving

sons taught
to be bold
to be loud
to explore
to take space
to be served
to expect
to demand
to inherit

in so many families
parents fear for daughters
and encourage sons
fear becomes control
encouragement becomes entitlement
girls managed
boys unleashed

the emotional burden on girls
begins early
they learn to notice
everyone's feelings
smooth tension
sense danger
mediating conflict
comforting siblings
listening to parents
being the peacekeepers
the stabilisers
the ones who hold the family
together

girls become
the emotional infrastructure
of the household
built from expectation
not choice

meanwhile
sons learn
that their emotions
are problems to be avoided
burdens to be placed
on the nearest girl
sister
mother
friend
future partner

and then comes inheritance
literal
and invisible

sons inherit property
legacy
lineage
trust
authority
future

daughters inherit
obligation
guilt
caretaking
silence
uneven expectations

the emotional estate
divided unfairly
before anyone notices

caretaking becomes destiny
for so many daughters
they become the ones
who care for ageing parents
ill siblings
struggling relatives
because they always have
because families assume
because daughters are raised
to sacrifice
while sons are raised
to be supported

so much harm
happens quietly
not from hatred
but from tradition
habit
unexamined belief
love twisted
into inequality

and beneath the waves
mermaids grow up
in tidepools
where rules differ
for brothers and sisters

a mermaid daughter
told to swim gently
stay near the rocks
be graceful
be agreeable
be calm

a merman son
told to range widely
test currents
chase storms
explore trenches
claim the deep

mermaid daughters
taught to read tides
to help
to soothe
to carry
to host gatherings
to sing for others
to serve the pod

merman sons
praised
for strength
for daring
for the same traits
their sisters
are scolded for

the tidepools reveal
how early this begins
how subtle
how soft
how devastating

mermaid girls
learn to shrink their songs
mermaid boys
learn that the ocean
belongs to them

but the sea
holds memory
older than these rules

the waves
do not recognise gender
the currents
do not reward entitlement
the storms
do not obey patriarchy
the deep
holds power
in all its forms

and mermaid daughters
begin to swim out
beyond the rules
beyond the shallows
into their own oceans

and human daughters
are doing the same

they unlearn
what families taught them
they reclaim space
they refuse caretaking
as destiny
they name harm
they demand equity
they protect their sons
and daughters differently
than they were protected

they refuse
to build new tidepools
with old rules

and the sea
applauds
every act of rebellion
every refusal
every woman
who steps out of the script
written for her
by family tradition

the tide turns
because daughters
turn it

motherhood and reproductive coercion

in these waters
motherhood is not only love
it is politics
pressure
expectation
it is the tide society tries to control
the womb treated as public property
the body treated as a resource
a landscape governed by others

the politics of pregnancy
begin long before conception
in whispers
in questions
in assumptions
when are you having children
why aren't you having children
why are you having more
why are you having less
a thousand inquiries masquerading as care
but heavy as chains

abortion access
the storm beneath the surface
a woman's right to her own body
treated as debate
as battleground
as theology
as moral test
as something strangers can vote on
as something men can legislate
as something governments can restrict
because control
is always the point

birth trauma
the wreckage hidden under polite baby showers
stories swallowed
teeth clenched
women dismissed as emotional
dramatic
fragile
while their bodies bear the scars
of medicalisation
intervention
violence
rushed decisions
ignored pleas
pain denied
pain minimised
pain normalised

the medicalisation of women's bodies
the endless monitoring
probing
testing
pathologising
the belief that the female body
is dangerous
unpredictable
needing supervision
names written on clipboards
while women lie open
exposed
silenced
gritting through procedures
done without consent
or with only the illusion of choice

society claims ownership over the womb
as if it were communal land
a reproduction farm
a national asset
men in parliament declaring
what is moral
what is allowed
what is forbidden
leaders urging women to birth for the economy
while offering no childcare
no flexible work
no healthcare
no safety
no future

women pay the price
in blood
in time
in bone heavy exhaustion
in careers derailed
in poverty
in shame

those who choose motherhood
are judged
those who do not choose motherhood
are judged
those who cannot conceive
are judged
those who terminate
are condemned
there is no path
that does not invite scrutiny

and beneath all of this
the oldest myth
mermaids as life bringers
fertile
mysterious
creatures of creation
bearers of new worlds
their magic celebrated
their autonomy erased
their reproductive power
mythologised
but never respected

men worship the symbol
and ignore the reality
ignore the danger
the fatigue
the labour
the trauma
the wonder
the cost

mermaids swim in these currents
carrying stories of women
whose pregnancies were forced
or forbidden
whose children were taken
whose choices were stolen
women trapped in marriages
trapped in laws
trapped in expectations
trapped in silence

mermaids feel the drag
of reproductive coercion
the heavy net of patriarchal desire
that demands babies
but refuses to support mothers
that demands purity
but refuses to respect autonomy
that demands sacrifice
without offering sanctuary

and still
women make choices
with courage
with clarity
with love
with fear
with resistance

they claim their bodies
they claim their wombs
they claim their desires
they claim the right
to decide what grows within them
or does not

the tide is shifting
slowly
relentlessly
toward bodily autonomy
toward truth
toward the end of silence
toward a world
where women are not vessels
not incubators
not symbols
not property
but sovereign beings
choosing freely
without apology

mermaids rise
life bringers
yes
but life owners too
their bodies not myths
not metaphors
not battlegrounds
their bodies theirs

and the ocean
holds them
in full respect

myth of the strong woman

society loves
the strong woman
adores her
celebrates her
quotes her
posts her
praises her resilience
her grit
her endurance

but only
because her strength
is useful
to everyone but her

the strong woman
is expected
to carry burdens
no one else will touch
to hold families together
to soothe partners
to raise children
to care for elders
to excel at work
to endure misogyny
to survive violence
to rise again
and again
and again

her strength
is treated as a resource
something to mine
to extract
to exploit
endlessly

the world demands
her competence
her calm
her caretaking
her capacity
her forgiveness
her labour
her emotional fluency

and offers her
nothing in return

no rest
no relief
no reciprocity
no safety
no softness
no place
to collapse

instead
she is asked
why she is so tired
why she is overwhelmed
why she is burnt out
why she cannot carry
just a little more

the strong woman
becomes a myth
a trap
a compliment
sharpened like a blade

because if she is strong
she cannot be struggling
if she is strong
she cannot need help
if she is strong
she cannot be a victim
if she is strong
she cannot break

strong becomes
an obligation
not a trait

and when she finally
crumbles
under the load
they ask her
what went wrong
as if strength
was supposed
to make her superhuman

beneath the waves
mermaids know
this myth well

the ocean worships
their power
their stamina
their speed
their endurance

mermaids carry
shipwrecks
on their backs
without complaint
dragging broken hulls
out of migration paths
salvaging debris
from storms
protecting coral
from destruction

they tow injured dolphins
shield fragile hatchlings
fight predators
calm tempests

yet they too
are asked
why they are tired
why they are not
always graceful
always available
always unshakable

their strength
is romanticised
weaponised
used to deny them
the right to rest
to mourn
to falter
to sink

but even mermaids
have limits
even mermaids
need the quiet
of deep water
need to let their tails
go still
need to float
without carrying
an entire world

and women
human women
are beginning to reject
the myth
of the strong woman

they are learning
that strength
should not mean
self abandonment
that resilience
should not be required
to survive
ordinary life

they are learning
to ask for help
to refuse burdens
to set boundaries
to rest
to soften
to collapse
to be human

they are learning
that strength
is not the absence
of need
but the presence
of self worth

mermaids rise
to meet them
showing with their bodies
their scars
their pauses
that no creature
born of tide and bone
can live
without rest

that strength
must be shared
not demanded
that resilience
must be supported
not exploited

the myth
of the strong woman
is fading
with the old tide

what is emerging
is something truer
and infinitely more powerful

a woman
who chooses
when to rise
when to rest
when to fight
when to float

a woman
who is strong
because she is free
not because she is carrying
what no one else will

mythology of the dangerous woman

for as long as stories
have been told
men have needed
a monster
in a woman's shape

from witches to sirens to mermaids
they carved myths
like weapons
sharpened on fear
bathed in control
polished with violence

the dangerous woman
appears in every age
every empire
every scripture
every whispered tale

a woman who speaks
becomes a witch
a woman who refuses
becomes a temptress
a woman who desires
becomes a seductress
a woman who thinks
becomes a threat

stories weaponised
to teach obedience
stories weaponised
to justify harm
stories weaponised
to make sure women
never gather too much power
never claim their full selves
never walk unafraid

witches burned
so women would fear knowledge
sirens demonised
so women would fear voice
mermaids rewritten
so women would fear freedom

the mythmakers knew
that to control a woman
you must first control
the story about her

call her dangerous
and you can cage her
call her monstrous
and you can silence her
call her seductive
and you can blame her
call her wicked
and you can punish her

this mythology
is ancient propaganda
a manual for patriarchy
cataloguing the ways
women become threats
simply by existing

witches
women with herbs
with healing
with community
with authority
torched
because men feared
what they could not own

sirens
singers
story keepers
warning shouters
not seducers
but survivors
who knew the dangers
of the sea
and the men who sailed it
turned into demons
because men needed
their failures
to be someone else's fault

mermaids
sovereign creatures
free moving
unclaimed
untamed
refusing marriage
refusing mastery
rewritten
as violent seductresses
who lure men to their deaths

but the truth
was always simpler
men drowned
in their own entitlement
and needed a myth
so they would not
see themselves

the dangerous woman
is a myth
that expands
whenever a woman expands

a woman too smart
dangerous
a woman too strong
dangerous
a woman too sexual
dangerous
a woman not sexual enough
dangerous
a woman who leads
dangerous
a woman who disobeys
dangerous
a woman who survives
dangerous

because patriarchy
cannot tolerate women
who are ungoverned

and beneath the water
mermaids roll their eyes
at the centuries of lies
told about them

they were never dangerous
they were free
and freedom
is the one thing
patriarchy fears most

so mermaids
kept their own stories
beneath the waves
of rebellion
and truth

stories where
witches rise
sirens resist
mermaids refuse
and a dangerous woman
means a woman
who will not bow

mermaids remember
how myths were used
to punish autonomy
to control the tide
of female power
to justify violence
and the deep
still hums
with those memories

yet still
women rise
witches reclaim their fire
sirens reclaim their voices
mermaids reclaim their depth
their danger
redefined
as strength

the only thing
truly dangerous
is a story
that teaches girls
to fear themselves

but the tide
is turning
women rewriting every myth
line by line
wave by wave

and the world
will learn
a dangerous woman
is simply a woman
who refuses
to be controlled

in the first years of the covid nineteen storm
twenty twenty
twenty twenty one
twenty twenty two
connection became a lifebuoy
a glowing buoy in dark water
technology tossing thin ropes between us
so we would not drift alone into the swell

yet every time we looked out across the world
we saw waves hitting other shores harder
we saw floods of grief elsewhere
while here in australia
we floated in comparative calm
safe bays
sheltered coves
luxuries still within reach
while millions of others battled riptides
and sank beneath unequal waves

the early lockdowns churned our closest waters
currents shifting beneath friendships
family lines splitting like fault lines
values rearranging like sand after a storm surge
boundaries rising like cliffs
showing us what behaviour could not be allowed
some ties snapping
others dissolving in the salt

women were swept deeper into caring roles
pulled down by undertows of responsibility
home schooling by day
working long hours in feminised professions
by night
aged care
nursing
cleaning
retail
all the invisible labour that keeps the ship afloat
yet is rarely seen from the captain's deck

survival meant some women were trapped
in homes that felt more like sinking wrecks
unsafe currents swirling behind locked doors
danger swelling with each hour of confinement

the pandemic magnified inequity
like sunlight refracting through deep water
showing every fracture
every inequality
gender
race
class
language
the layers of identity shaping
who could reach the surface
and who was dragged under

when child care closed
when schools shut like storm shutters
women relinquished income
dreams
ambitions
to hold families steady
to keep children floating
to keep households from capsizing

flight attendants lost their skies
hospitality workers their harbours
the travel industry vanished beneath a wave
and so many women lost their livelihoods with it
universities closed their borders
but government cast its lifeline
only to mining and construction
male dominated industries
lashed safely to the mast
while university women
casual academics
researchers
artists
were left treading water
until their strength gave out

healthcare workers
mostly women
were the mermaids of this storm
unable to retreat
unable to hide
swimming into danger
delivering care

carrying exhaustion
like heavy kelp around their ribs
holding the nation's breath
in their cupped hands

women faced the double tide
paid work rolling in
unpaid work crashing over it
cleaning
cooking
teaching
soothing
managing
mending
day after day
wave after wave
their mental health eroding
like soft cliffs under relentless surf

gendered poverty sharpened like coral
women already earning less
already holding part time
precarious
low paid jobs
found themselves sliced by new hardship
first nations women
women of colour
women with disabilities
all pushed closest to rocks

lost hours
lost jobs
lost stability
translated to hunger
to fear
to quiet panic
echoing through coastal towns
city towers
suburban kitchens

and as in every disaster
violence rose like a hidden rip
dragging women into deeper peril
intimate partner abuse
sexual assault
emotional cruelty
all rising behind closed doors
while shelters
already fragile hulls
were forced to cut capacity
or close entirely
leaving women adrift in stormwater
with nowhere safe to swim

other support systems frayed in the wind
job programs
poverty relief
arts organisations
all battered by the gale

diverse women rowed the frontline
nurses
caregivers
cleaners
mothers and aunties
grandmothers holding communities together
their hands raw from gripping oars
their bodies cold from constant exposure
their courage the only lighthouse we had

yet government recognition remained shallow
universities denied jobkeeper
artists abandoned
women in precarious roles forgotten
while the mining giants
the construction kings
and retailers like harvey norman
were kept warm and dry behind reinforced walls

the pandemic cast a hard light across the ocean
revealing the reef structures of gender
inequality
the deep trenches of violence
the tidal drag of poverty
the fragile boats that women must captain alone

and the current whispered one truth
efforts to build a gender equal australia
are not optional
they are the only way
to keep us afloat
when the next storm comes

very early on we learn to lose at chess
we learn that our victories must be softened
we learn that we are not mates
and so we are shut out
of that great australian virtue
that circle of elbows and laughter and power
mateship
that unspoken law
that invisible gate

and so it begins
the first tide pulling us back
before we even know how to swim

and then one woman rose
julia gillard
twenty seventh prime minister of australia
first and only so far
her leadership held with strength and reason
yet met with scorn sharpened by gender
examined not for policy but for her body
her choices
her unmarried life
her childless life
her womanhood
as though each was a flaw
a crack
a reason to doubt her right
to stand where she stood

the media hurled its contempt
the opposition hurled its lines
the internet seethed with filth
pornographic images
degrading insults
a whole storm of misogyny
trying to drag her under

and on the ninth of October
two thousand and twelve
julia answered
her voice a current no man could block
naming what they feared she would name
that sexism rationalises the patriarchy
and misogyny enforces it
that power protects itself
that contempt has teeth
that hatred grows in darkness

australia needs
a national integrity commission
a body with courage and claws
to investigate corruption
to shine light on misconduct
to hold public hearings like a royal commission
to tear open the shadows
where the boys club hides

to lift standards
and end the quiet favouring
of mates mates mates
as though governance is a pub back room
as though women are never at the table

without such a commission
there are no consequences
no anchors for truth
no accountability for ministerial misconduct
or sexual harassment
no reckoning for the scandals
of twenty twenty two
the community sports grants
the commuter car parks
the leppington triangle land purchase
each one a reminder
that when power polices itself
women are left unprotected
the public is left uninformed
and democracy becomes a leaking boat

here in this story telling
the water is political
the tide is gendered
and the question rises
like a dorsal fin beneath the surface
how do women swim
in a system built to drown them

in the patriarchal ocean
misogyny does not strike only one shore
it hits all who are read as woman
all who move through the world
with femininity in their currents
all who carry softness
fluidity
vulnerability
or beauty
whether they claim womanhood
reject it
expand it
or redefine it

queer misogyny
is the storm within the storm
the violence reserved
for lesbian women
bisexual women
trans women
non binary femmes
anyone whose existence
refuses the straight line
anyone whose life
disrupts the neat categories
patriarchy demands

lesbian women face misogyny
for loving women
for refusing male entitlement
for building whole worlds
without men at the centre
their love treated as threat
their autonomy mocked
their existence pornified
or erased
men furious
not because they are excluded
but because they are irrelevant

bisexual women face misogyny
for being fluid
desired by men
yet distrusted by them
desired by women
yet dismissed by both
accused of confusion
or promiscuity
punished for attraction
seen as always available
never committed
as if love itself
needs to be straight
to be believed

trans women face misogyny
weaponised and sharpened
a combination of patriarchy
and transmisogyny
their womanhood policed
their identities questioned
their safety threatened
their lives debated
their existence politicised
their legitimacy denied
by those who fear
what they cannot control
who fear women
who were not shaped
in ways they understand
whose womanhood proves
how expansive womanhood truly is

non binary femmes face misogyny
for refusing binary scripts
for daring to shimmer
in between
for carrying femininity
without accepting the cage
that usually comes with it
punished for their fluidity
their refusal to be one thing
their refusal to be predictable
their refusal to be owned
their refusal to be named
by anyone but themselves

the patriarchal policing of identity
is relentless
anyone who disrupts hierarchy
is punished
anyone who embodies complexity
is mocked
anyone who refuses categorisation
is threatened
patriarchy relies
on neat boundaries
and queer existence
is beautifully
devastatingly
boundaryless

beneath these tides
mermaids swim
creatures of fluid gender
fluid form
fluid desire
they have never obeyed binaries
never belonged to the categories
land people worship
their bodies shifting with the moon
their identities moving
with the currents
their beauty uncontained
their desire abundant
their existence
a contradiction patriarchy cannot hold

and so
they are punished
feared
mocked
flattened into myths
stripped of complexity
reduced to seduction
or danger
their multiplicity erased

because mermaids prove
that the world is not binary
never has been
never will be
because they show
that gender is not fixed
nor singular
nor owned by men
because they reveal
how much freedom
patriarchy has stolen

queer women
queer femmes
trans women
non binary people
live closest to the truth
that womanhood
is not one thing
not one shape
not one history
not one body
not one story

and queer misogyny
exists precisely because
patriarchy knows
its entire structure
could collapse
under the weight
of queer truth

mermaids rise
in their fluid forms
their shimmering refusal
their defiant tenderness
their ungovernable beauty
they carry the stories
of all those punished
for not fitting

they whisper
you are sacred
because you are not binary
because you do not conform
because you live your truth
in a world that punishes truth

queer misogyny is real
and relentless
but so is queer resilience
queer joy
queer brilliance
queer strength

and somewhere in the deep
mermaids gather
around those who have been harmed
singing a song
that sounds like healing
and rebellion
and freedom

the waves crash harder here
against altars
against pulpits
against the carved stone certainty
of patriarchal faith
for patriarchy assumes
that men are made to lead
and women are made to serve
cooperative and reproductive subordinates
vessels
followers
never the ones who speak to god

these assumptions surface everywhere
but nowhere so violently
as in religion
in the faiths that treat women
as though they are lesser
as though equality is heresy
as though divinity speaks in only one voice
and it is male

we read it in sacred texts
across all persuasions
written in eras where women were property
and still interpreted
as if those eras never ended
we see it in iconic imagery
the gods male
the prophets male
the leaders male
the saviours male
and when a woman appears
she is virgin
or whore
or mother
never sovereign

religious taboos about women's sexuality
layered thick
shame as doctrine
purity as prison
desire as sin
pleasure as corruption
her body framed as threat
as temptation
as wound
as warning

and all religious institutions
still run by men
councils of men
rulings by men
scriptures interpreted by men
traditions policed by men
the absence of women's voices
becoming a theological earthquake
the ground of belief tilted
because half of humanity
has never been allowed
to steer the spiritual ship

the lack of input from women
has shaped the world profoundly
misogynistic readings
sanctioned by centuries
passed through civilisations
codified into culture
into law
into punishment
into ritual
into silence

men dominate religious institutions
and use them as measuring sticks
deciding whether women
can preach
or pray aloud
or lead
or interpret
or step onto the sacred platform
men as gatekeepers
men as arbiters
men deciding where the divine begins
and where women end

religion
which can be a force for good
becomes mired
in ideologies of exclusion
bigotry layered on bigotry
especially toward women
who are deemed
second class souls
second class citizens
barred from innumerable rights
their male counterparts
receive automatically

euphemisms such as family ideals
used like velvet gloves
to disguise iron control
preserving heteronormative
sexist gender roles
wrapping restriction
in language of holiness

and whenever women challenge
male spiritual authority
whether they claim a new faith
or reinterpret the old
their voices are treated
as political threats
not theological insights
their courage punished
their autonomy feared

the response has always been the same
shun them
silence them
banish them
label them dangerous
label them heretic
label them enemy
destroy them if necessary

for centuries
women have been stoned
burned at the stake
executed in honour killings
murdered for spiritual daring
tortured for questioning
erased for speaking
made examples of
so others would stay quiet

yet women have always
displayed enormous piety
enormous spiritual force
in every religion
every culture
every era

and still
male authorities tried to tame them
contain their faith
domesticate their devotion
shrink their radiance
into something safe
something compliant
something that would never
challenge the throne

but beneath these violent doctrines
beneath the patriarchal tide
mermaids churn
sacred daughters of the deep
unholy to the men who fear them
holy to the ocean that raised them
their spirituality tidal
untamed
ancient
a direct line to the divine
that no institution can sever

they rise in fierce waves
against the idea
that god is male
that truth is male
that authority is male
that holiness flows
only through patriarchal hands

mermaids know
that spirituality belongs to everyone
that the divine is not property
that faith is not a hierarchy
that women's voices
have always held the power
to reshape the world

and the waves
keep crashing

resilience
is not what they told us
not endless endurance
not absorbing harm
not carrying more
than any body should

resilience
is refusal
is uprising
is imagining a world
that has not existed yet
and stepping toward it
wave by wave

women reclaiming the world
mermaids reclaiming the ocean
the work is parallel
the tide is the same

after all these chapters
after all the storms
after all the truths spoken
and salt shed
and wounds mapped
there comes a moment
when the current shifts
toward what comes next

women are reclaiming
what was taken
their names
their bodies
their wages
their joy
their places under the sun
their safe nights
their loud voices
their art
their choices
their futures

they are no longer
simply surviving misogyny
they are rewriting the world
brick by brick
law by law
tide by tide

and beneath the waves
mermaids rise
resilient from centuries
of misstorying
of mythmaking
of being twisted
into symbols they never were

they reclaim the ocean
its reefs
its trenches
its sacred currents
its ancestral memory
its future

they turn their voices
into instruments of change
songs that soften storms
or redirect currents
songs that call whales home
songs that warn predators
songs that teach the young
there is another way
to live in the deep

mermaids are architects
of a new sea
women are architects
of a new world

future tides
carry something different
something quieter
gentler
stronger
cleaner

in the future
girls do not shrink
to fit beside boys
women do not lose careers
to keep the peace
no one is harmed
for saying no
any ocean
any home
is safe to swim in

in the future
climate justice
is not optional
care work
is valued
housing
is secure
survival
is not gendered
power
is not hoarded
masculinity
is not threatened
by equality

in the future
there are no myths
that punish women
for being whole
no stories
that cage them
in beauty
in obedience
in silence

in the future
mermaids rise openly
their truths no longer twisted
their power no longer feared
their bodies no longer claimed
their songs no longer misused

they swim
without shrinking
take up the whole water
tail shining
voice ringing
free

and women
do the same
on land

resilience
is no longer
what keeps them alive
it becomes instead
what allows them
to build
to dream
to thrive

future tides
are coming
not because they arrive
on their own
but because women
and mermaids
together
create them

and when those tides arrive
they bring with them
a world
no longer shaped
by misogyny

but by liberation

in this continent of broken agreements
the ground holds stories older than language
older than conquest
older than the men who came to tear it open
yet the toxic masculinity
of mining and construction
continues to drill into country
as if earth were an enemy
as if stone were beneath dignity
as if landscape were resource
not relative

corporations
assure environment and heritage bodies
that no harm will be done
that sacred sites will be safe
that protections will hold
while in back rooms
they lobby the coalition
with maps marked for extraction
with schematics for blasting
with quiet promises of profit

and when things accidentally go wrong
when a cave is destroyed
when a river is poisoned
when a forest is erased
a handful of dollars is tossed forward
called compensation
as if land can be repaid
as if culture can be refunded
as if gaia keeps receipts

australia has weak laws
weak teeth
weak consequences
for destroying declared environment
and heritage sites
because capitalism calls destruction
development
and men in high offices nod along

we do not value native habitats
not the eucalyptus forests
not the grasslands
not the mangroves
not the wetlands
not the deserts blooming at dusk
we forget
that these places
give us what we cannot live without
ecosystem services

the quiet labour of the living world
filtering water
cooling air
steadying soil
protecting us from storms
and flooding
and heat
and drought
holding the world together
while we pretend their worth is optional

environment groups are demonised
not because they are wrong
but because they challenge capitalism
because they dare to say
that endless growth is a myth
that taking without returning is theft
that the land is not a wallet

australia's response needs to be courage
stop wholesale land clearing
maintain environmental flows
reconnect the interrupted corridors
linking national parks
and reserves
protect threatened grasslands
as fiercely as forests
end fracking
end the ripping apart of aquifers
end the torching of country
that cannot be reborn under concrete

but the mining industry carries its own violence
a culture sharpened by toxic masculinity
a roughness worn like armour
where harassment is common
where misogyny is background noise
where positions of power are abused
where codes of conduct are decoration
and cover ups are tradition

the risks to workers are many
but for women
the risks multiply
the danger thickens
the harassment is accepted
overlooked
laughed off
dismissed
woven into the culture like dust

women report eating meals
beside adult magazines
open
normalised
as if the workplace were a boy's club
not an industry
as if their discomfort did not matter
as if their humanity did not matter

harassment is routine
misogyny predictable
violence a shadow
following women through mine sites
through donga corridors
through shifts that stretch into night

resource extraction and masculinity
are fused in australia
a belief that land must be conquered
that rocks must submit
that rivers must bow
that country must be punctured
split
opened
emptied

and that women too
must endure
must soften
must shrink
must not complain
must not disrupt the masculine myth

but mermaids rise from flooded pits
from dammed rivers
from tailings ponds leaching into creeks
their tails streaked with sediment
their hair matted with dust
they carry messages from the underground
from the aquifers
from the roots of stringybarks
from ancestors singing beneath the soil

they say
the land is alive
the water is alive
the women are alive
and none of this is yours to take
without consequence

the future of this continent
depends on listening
to the earth
to the women
to the oceans
to the grasslands
to the ancient places calling us back

because extraction without care
is not strength
it is collapse
it is cowardice
it is the loudest confession
of a culture that fears
what it cannot dominate

science and knowledge production

science
the supposed home
of objectivity
rationality
precision
truth

yet for centuries
its halls have echoed
with the erasure
of women knowledge holders

knowledge
is not neutral
it is shaped
by who is allowed
to speak
to explore
to record
to publish
to be believed

from traditional herbalists
centuries of women
who learned the language
of plants
the secrets of roots
the medicine of leaves
the healing of moon cycles
the chemistry of soil
and sickness
and birth
their expertise
dismissed as superstition
their remedies stolen
their names erased
their bodies punished
through witch hunts
discrediting
banishment
violence

their brilliance
made dangerous
because it existed
outside the control
of men

to modern researchers
women in laboratories
women in field stations
women in observatories
designing experiments
collecting data
publishing breakthroughs
yet rarely credited
rarely cited
rarely funded
their discoveries claimed
their contributions minimised
their genius framed
as assistance
instead of authorship

women locked out
of senior positions
peer review
tenure tracks
awards
grants
professional respect

the myth persists
that science progresses
through great men
when in truth
it has advanced
on the backs
of stolen data
borrowed labour
and silenced women

and to first nations women scientists
whose sky land and sea expertise
is older than any white institution
whose astronomical knowledge
mapped constellations
long before telescopes
whose ecological systems thinking
held balance
between species
between water cycles
between fire and regrowth
between harvesting and caring
between seasons
and survival

whose languages
carry encoded science
botany
meteorology
navigation
geology
oceanography

yet whose knowledge
is ignored
dismissed
deemed unscientific
not because it isn't science
but because patriarchy
and colonialism
cannot comprehend
science without ownership
science without domination
science without hierarchy

mermaids swim
in parallel
carrying generational wisdom
passed from tide to tide
from grandmother to granddaughter
the ways of currents
the habits of whales
the migrations of fish
the patterns of storms
the medicine of sea grass
the taste of changing salinity
the meaning of coral colour

they hold libraries
in their bodies
maps
in their blood
archives
in their memory

but men
who have never touched saltwater
never listened to the hum
of the tide
never learned from the dark
never respected the deep
dismiss this wisdom
as myth
as fantasy
as nothing

because patriarchy
cannot accept
that women
or mermaids
or first nations custodians
or traditional healers
hold knowledge
that existed
long before men claimed
to have invented
science

the ocean laughs
at this arrogance
the stars sigh
at this ignorance
the land grows weary
of being ignored
by those who think
knowledge is something
they created

mermaids swim
toward the truth
women rise
toward the truth
first nations scientists
teach
the truth

knowledge
is older than patriarchy
and bigger
than the men
who tried to gatekeep it

and women
are reclaiming
their place
in the lineage of knowing

in the deep
mermaids whisper
to every girl
every woman
every knowledge keeper

you are the scientist
you are the scholar
you are the archive
you are the evidence
you are the truth

in these waters
mermaids have only one sanctioned shape
one story
one image permitted by the surface world
they must be seduction
danger wrapped in beauty
temptation with flowing hair
their power reduced to lure
song
skin
their depth erased
their history stripped
their autonomy rewritten
until the ocean's daughters
become only what sailors feared
or wanted
or wanted to conquer

and on land
women are given the same narrow script
smile
soften
appease
look pleasant
stay unthreatening
fit your whole self inside
the smallest possible outline

the workplace echoes this confinement
ambitious women aren't leaders
they are bossy
aggressive
too much
too sharp
too driven
while men with the same traits
are celebrated as visionaries
go getters
natural candidates for upper management
rewarded for the very qualities
women are punished for

so women adjust
language softened
edges rounded
attire formal and careful
tone lowered
anger swallowed
brilliance translated into safety
womanhood shaped to avoid backlash
to survive inside male dominated currents

and still
the microaggressions come
passive aggressive remarks
unwanted touching
hands brushing too close
jokes not jokes

comments disguised as compliments
tension coiling beneath every interaction
each moment accumulated like silt
affecting focus
productivity
exhaustion

and the most common of all
smile

women smile their way through meetings
through hallways
through shop floors
through cafes
through boardrooms
through life
taught to appear unthreatening
as if their existence is a service
as if their purpose is to please men

women who do not smile
are considered strange
unlikeable
hostile
unfeminine
their competence irrelevant
their humanity ignored
the smile treated as the true measure

smiling becomes gendered labour
a performance
a mask
a ritual of appeasement
a concession to unequal power
where women contort their faces
so that men feel comfortable

men are almost never told to smile
because men are seen as subjects
women as scenery

when a man tells a woman to smile
the message is clear
you exist to please me
change your appearance for me
bend your expression for me
i hold authority over your body
your mood
your face

a toxic manager telling a woman to smile
demands conformity
to the fantasised version of femininity
the docile
pleasing
beautiful front facing woman
stripped of political agency
stripped of valid emotion

and the response
the internal response
ranges from anger
to humiliation
to frustration
to the hollow ache of being unseen

yet women keep smiling
because it is safer
appeasement is safer
unthreatening is safer
survival often means swallowing truth
until it becomes bone

and girls learn early
that the demand to smile
is the first lesson in becoming small
a kind of cultural declawing
a depoliticising force
making girls docile
keeping them quiet
distracted from the deeper political issues
from the exploitation they face
from the climate crisis
from the epidemic
of missing and murdered
first nations girls and women
from every injustice disguised beneath the grin

women grit their teeth
and smile their way through workplaces
relationships
shops
streets
public transport
public life

and everywhere
pop culture reinforces the story
music
movies
shows
video games
teaching men and boys
that women are objects
property
ornaments
rewards
reinforcing the myth
that they hold less value
that their pain matters less
that their bodies belong to others

and from this small stuff
from every boys will be boys shrug
grows a code of silence
in which sexual violence thrives unchecked
because if the small harms are tolerated
the larger harms take root

most children's books still place girls
as passive
secondary
waiting to be saved
boys as heroes
adventurers
leaders
girls learning their place before they can speak
boys learning entitlement before they can read

and when women stand up for themselves
they are accused of victimhood
told to toughen up
called soft
weak
hysterical
yet there is nothing soft
nothing weak
nothing hysterical
about confronting harassment
about demanding safety
about challenging violence
it takes a kind of toughness
few men will ever be asked to know

women downplay their own suffering
because they know others have it worse
and they are taught
not to make a fuss
not to complain
not to misinterpret
not to feel too strongly
not to embarrass anyone
even themselves

they ask
was i asking for it
because society taught them to
because voices around them
dismiss
minimise
belittle
pretend they are overreacting

australia
like the world
is built around men
and feminism is demonised
precisely because it threatens this structure
because it asks men to loosen their grip
on authority

and yet
research shows
harmful gender stereotypes begin early
but collective action
can change the story

it takes action
legislation
funding
courage

social justice and environmental care
rethinking family
defending non traditional forms of kinship
championing the outcast
uplifting the unheard
challenging patriarchal control
these are the foundations of change

since the nineteen seventies
we have said
teach daughters to mow lawns
check the oil
earn their own money
teach sons to cook
clean
do laundry
basic life skills
not gender roles

yet still
girls are taught
to accept
to suppress
to swallow
to absorb
to carry the weight of sexism
to become the smiling mermaids
men want
instead of the fierce sea women
they are

on the surface
mermaids are seduction
below
they are storms
currents
depth
ancient power
their image has been caged
but they themselves
remain wild

and women
on land
are the same

sports misogyny

in stadiums
arenas
courts
fields
gyms
and digital spaces
women athletes move
with power
precision
discipline
grit
and still
misogyny follows them
like a shadow
they never invited

the pay gaps
are oceanic
vast as trenchwater
absurd in their scale
women doing the same work
more work
harder work
with less reward
less sponsorship
less broadcast time
less investment
less respect

their victories
are celebrated briefly
their failures
magnified
their bodies judged
before their performances
their muscles questioned
their strength mocked
their femininity interrogated

an entire culture
afraid of strong women
afraid of speed
afraid of power
afraid of the sight
of women who refuse
to break
to bend
to shrink

women's leagues
dismissed as lesser
despite skill
despite strategy
despite brilliance
despite statistics
despite the thousands
who show up
every single week
to watch them rise

yet still
the funding lags
the scheduling is unfair
the commentary patronising
the abuses rampant
the doubt relentless

online abuse
is a sport of its own
men hurling insults
threats
slurs
as if athleticism
is an affront
as if excellence
is a provocation
as if women in motion
disrupt the world order
they cling to

women in sport
stand in storms
of harassment
sexualisation
racism
transphobia
and a constant demand
to justify
their existence

as if competition
belongs only to men
as if strength
is a gendered right
as if sweat
belongs to one body
not another

and beneath the surface
in deeper waters
mermaids rise
athletes of the deep
born of currents
trained by tides

they swim faster
than sailors ever dreamed
they turn sharper
than any rudder
they sprint through turbulence
with power that bends
the water around them

their bodies are built
for endurance
for speed
for ferocity
for grace
for survival
for victory

and yet
in the stories told above
their athleticism becomes
seduction
danger
myth

their power recast
as weapon
their speed reframed
as lure
their strength mistranslated
into enchantment

because patriarchy
cannot imagine
a female creature
stronger
faster
more capable
than a man

but mermaids
know their own bodies
their own stamina
their own might
they race with storms
they dance with whales
they outrun sharks
they rise through whirlpools
with ease

they are the original athletes
the unacknowledged champions
the goddesses of endurance
and velocity

and above
human women mirror them
running
jumping
lifting
fighting
striking
sprinting
diving
skating
climbing
rising

they are not asking
for permission
they are not asking
for approval
they are not asking
to be liked

they are claiming
what should have always been theirs
a place in the arena
a place in the water
a place at the start line
a place at the summit
a place on the podium

they are redefining
what strength looks like
what competition feels like
what victory means

and the world
is changing
slowly
reluctantly
but inevitably
around their footsteps
their strokes
their kicks
their flights

beneath the waves
the mermaids cheer
women athletes rising
like tides
that no one
can turn back

sustainable fashion and capitalist pressure

in this century of fast commerce
scientists warn that human population
and the weight of our habits
have bent the climate off course
greenhouse gases rising from fossil fuels
forests cut down
oceans warming
the planet thinning under our demands

and woven through all of it
another river of waste flows silently
fashion
the churn of garments
stitched quickly
sold cheaply
discarded instantly
each year millions of tonnes of clothes
produced
worn
thrown away
every second
a rubbish truck of fabric burnt or buried
the landfills swelling like toxic dunes
the smoke rising like a warning
the earth saying
i cannot hold this much any longer

australia sits at the top of this textile hill
our closets overflowing
our bins fuller still
garments pouring into landfills
leaching dyes
chemicals
synthetic particles
the land choking beneath polyester rain

and the ocean
always the final keeper of our mistakes
fills with microfibres
tiny threads of plastic drifting through waves
invisible wounds in the water
absorbed by fish
carried by currents
eaten by whales
rising back into our own bodies
a loop we refuse to see
even as it enters the blood

this is not accidental
this is capitalism shaping women
pressuring them to look a certain way
to consume constantly
to update wardrobes
to chase trends
that sprint ahead each season

telling women
your worth is visual
your value is surface
your acceptability
changes with the colour palette

women know the truth
they want clothes that are comfortable
attractive
and have pockets
real pockets
not symbolic ones
not decorative lies
but space to hold their lives

and still the industry refuses
because pockets imply power
autonomy
function
not decoration
and fashion has long treated women's clothing
as spectacle
not tool

but change is coming
slow at first
like the tide at dawn
a circular economy for fashion
creating better garments
better services
better systems

regenerating the environment
prioritising the rights and equity
of everyone in the fashion chain
from grower
to spinner
to dyer
to machinist
to wearer

a circular fashion industry
would distribute opportunity
make it diverse
inclusive
thriving
resilient
an ecosystem instead of a funnel
a community instead of a factory line

we need clothes designed to be used more
to last longer
to resist the churn
we need clothes made to be made again
reconstructed
repaired
reborn
we need clothes made from safe materials
recycled fibres
renewable textiles
the earth breathing easier
with each regenerative choice

when fashion becomes circular
we tackle the roots of global challenges
climate change
biodiversity loss
pollution
we soften the pressure on women
we slow the wheel of consumption
we honour the ocean
the land
the air

and in the water
mermaids watch
their tails brushing drifting fabric scraps
their hair tangled with microfibres
their bodies carrying the evidence
of our throwaway culture
they call to us
to reinvent fashion
to unlearn excess
to clothe ourselves in consciousness
not harm

in these tides
we realise the truth
that what we wear
is never only cloth
it is future
it is footprint
it is a choice with weight

and we cannot keep pretending
that the ocean will survive our wardrobes
if we do not change the way we make
and wear
and discard
what we call fashion

in these dark waters
the weapons trade rises like an oil slick
spreading across oceans
coating shorelines
blotting out futures
for decades
it is one of the most lucrative businesses
on earth
profits climbing predictably
year after year
as if destruction were a harvest
as if death were a commodity
as if human suffering were merely collateral
in the market of power

the ready availability of weapons
of ammunition
leads everywhere
to the same outcomes
ruined cities
shattered families
political repression
crime
terror settling over civilian populations
like a suffocating fog

irresponsible arms transfers
destabilise entire regions
enable violations of embargoes
fuel human rights abuses
and where violence takes root
development falters
investment withers
schools shutter
hospitals crumble
communities fracture

countries caught in conflict
or crushed beneath crime
struggle to reach even the most basic
internationally agreed development goals
for how can you build a future
when the present is burning

and now
we see it again
russia's aggression against ukraine
images flooding our homes
homes already full of too many tragedies
but these
show both human devastation
and environmental catastrophe
forests turned to ash
rivers poisoned
soil sown with landmines
the land wounded
long after the shells stop falling

and in gaza
the world watches
land reduced to rubble
children killed
families displaced
hospitals destroyed
water systems collapsed
the environment torn apart
the sea choking on debris
the air thick with dust
the land unable to breathe

war is not only a human disaster
it is an ecological one
the earth becomes a battlefield
the soil absorbs the trauma
the ocean carries the wreckage
the winds sweep away the smoke
the planet weeps with the people

beneath these waves
mermaids feel the shockwaves
echoes of bombs rippling through the deep
they watch as humanity
kills not only one another

but the very ecosystems required to live
they swim through waters contaminated
with fragments of conflict
steel
ash
shrapnel
the violent inheritance
of nations who profit from war

women around the world
work to end these conflicts
every day
they do not give up
even when walking into minefields
of politics
of ego
of patriarchal posturing
of men who treat war as theatre
and peace as an afterthought

women negotiate
women rebuild
women bury the dead
women tend the wounded
women demand diplomacy
women hold communities together
through collapse
through terror
through devastation

they know
that weapons make widows
and orphans
that war consumes the labour of generations
that peace is not granted
it is made
stitched together
day by day
by hands willing to hold the world gently

and still
the trade continues
guns shipped
bombs sold
drones launched
contracts signed
wealth accumulated by those far removed
from the blast zones
from the blood
from the grief

this story telling asks
what kind of civilisation
chooses profit
over people
over land
over oceans
over the future

and it answers
quietly
through the mermaids rising from the deep
only a broken one

war wounds the world
war wounds women
war wounds the very waters we depend on

and until the weapons trade is confronted
regulated
dismantled
there can be no true peace
no safe shore
no healed ocean

yet women keep working
keep fighting
keep hoping
keep rising

they are the tide
turning slowly
steadily
against the machinery of war

in every corner of the creative world
misogyny swims quietly
a current beneath the surface
altering what rises
what sinks
what survives

in publishing
women's manuscripts are read
through a male lens
their stories labelled niche
their protagonists unrelatable
their ambition excessive
their brilliance accidental
their genres ghettoised
their worth measured
by how well they imitate
the men who came before

women write
entire galaxies
entire revolutions
entire architectures of emotion
yet are reviewed less
marketed less
shortlisted less
paid less
archived less

their literary lineage
cut short by curators
who decide whose words
deserve memory

in film
women's stories are pitched
and passed over
deemed unprofitable
universal only when men speak
their roles limited
to love interest
dead wife
background girl
silent suffering
or manic pixie catalyst
for a man's transformation

female directors
fight for budgets
fight for credibility
fight to be heard on their own sets
their vision questioned
their authority doubted
their talent framed
as unexpected

in music
women write
compose
conduct
produce
yet are credited less
dismissed more
sexualised always

their voices scrutinised
their bodies controlled
their artistry overshadowed
by male collaborators
who take credit
take ownership
take space

in fine art
women paint masterpieces
in studios
in kitchens
in stolen hours
but galleries hang their work
rarely
quietly
if at all

male painters
claim innovation
while women
who invented the technique
are lost
in footnotes
auction catalogues
never printed

genius is not gendered
but recognition is

and beneath the waves
mermaids create
with a ferocity
older than language
singing entire oceans
into being
shaping coral
with the pitch of their voices
sculpting currents
with the sweep of their tails
composing symphonies
in whale song
and storm surge

yet even here
men find ways
to take the credit

stories told of them
twist their power
into temptation
their voice
into lure
their creativity
into danger
their autonomy
into myth

men claim
mermaids sing for them
when in truth
mermaids sing for themselves
for the tide
for the memory
for the deep

the patriarchal imagination
cannot tolerate
a woman
or a mermaid
whose art
exists independently
of male desire

so it reframes
their creation
as chaos
their brilliance
as witchcraft
their independence
as threat

but mermaids
keep creating
unbothered
unbroken

their art is saltwater memory
their craft
older than patriarchy
older than myth
older than the world
that tries to silence them

and human women
in studios
and rehearsal rooms
and small bedrooms
and borrowed offices
and late night cafés
mirror this truth

they write
they paint
they compose
they choreograph
they film
they sculpt
they design

and the world reshapes
itself around them
however slowly

misogyny in the arts
tries to dim the brilliance
but cannot
contain it

for every cut
women create more
for every dismissal
they rise higher
for every theft
they make new work

and below
in the deepest depths
mermaids gather
their songs weaving
through the bones of the sea
honouring the artists
who were forgotten
celebrating the ones
who survive
calling forth the voices
yet to come

their song says
create anyway
create loudly
create wildly
create without apology
create like the tide
that erases
and rebuilds
worlds

part two

mermaid tool kit

mermaid mantra
we rise together
we listen deeply
we believe women
we guard our boundaries
we lift each other's names
we refuse to compete
we rest without guilt
we honour every tide
we challenge harm with truth
we keep each other afloat

we rise together
we lift the tide for all

honouring the first tides

we acknowledge and honour
the first peoples of these lands and waters
their deep spiritual connection
their unbroken relationship with country

country that is landforms and waterways
sea and sky
trees and rocks
plants and animals
foods and medicines
minerals and sacred places
woven together as one living whole

we honour the water beings
the yawkyawk who dwell
in billabongs and springs
their presence ancient
their songs carried
through ripples and reflections
reminding us that country is alive
and has always been cared for
by those who know how to listen

we recognise country
as story and knowledge
as song and ceremony
as art and ancestry
as law and language
as every footstep
past present and future

we honour the custodians
who care for these lands
these coasts
these rivers
these oceans
who have always known
how to tend country
how to walk with it
how to speak its truth

we recognise their sovereignty
never ceded
their wisdom
never broken
their stories
never lost
carried forward like tides
steady and enduring

we pay our respects
to elders past and present
and to the generations rising
their voices strong
their knowledge deep
their connection flowing
like currents beneath all things

may this work
move gently upon their country
and may its words
honour the first storytellers
who have always
kept the tide alive

the tideline of wellbeing

being a feminist
is supporting women
all women
women from every culture
women in the workforce
women carving their own paths
women dreaming of lives
they have not yet been allowed to live

women do better together
this is the oldest magic we know
instead of tearing each other down

we can empower
encourage
inspire
we can lift each other
like waves lifting driftwood
like tides carrying small boats
like mermaids linking arms
and rising

be a supporter
of the women around you
the ones you work with
the ones you drink with
the ones you love
and the ones who do not yet know
they deserve love
the women not as fortunate
whose battles go unseen
and unheard

together
we can champion one another
together
we can become the best
we can be
a collective tide
a pod of mermaids
moving as one
through deep waters

but here is a warning
quiet and necessary

as women
we often say yes
out of obligation
out of fear
out of over commitment
out of wanting to be valued
or noticed
or accepted

we tuck away our boundaries
our courage
our pride
our self commitment
our time
our safety
to meet other people's expectations

we have been socialised
to believe our worth
is measured by what we give
how much we soften the world
for others
how much labour we absorb
how little we ask for
how beautifully we sacrifice

and so saying no
feels dangerous
like diminishing our own value
like stepping out of line
like refusing the script
written for us

but this toolkit
holds both truths

support other women
yes
lift other women
yes
stand with other women
always

and also
hold your boundaries
honour your energy
protect your time
preserve your safety
tend your own flame
so it does not burn out

because the strongest support
comes from women
who are not depleted
not erased
not exhausted
but whole

in this toolkit
we pass on the tools
we were never given

encouragement
solidarity
sisterhood
boundaries
courage
rest

all of it
all at once
all necessary
for the tides ahead

practical tactical tools

listen first
listen fully
listen beneath the words
the way a mermaid hears currents
shifting miles away
trust that women know their own tides

believe her
without interrogation
without the drag of doubt
let your faith in her voice
be the shoreline she can land on

name the harm
call it what it is
microaggression
misogyny
violence
silencing
naming turns shadows into shape
and shape into truth

share your resources
not scraps
but ropes
boats
maps
the things that have kept you afloat
in storms she might not yet have weathered

say her name in rooms she is not in
amplify her work
lift her reputation
let your words be currents
that carry her forward

stand beside her
in the meeting
in the protest
in the emergency
mermaids travel in pods
because survival is a collective art

hold space
space without judgement
without rushing her
without shrinking her feelings
the sea expands for those who need it

ask what she needs
not what you assume she needs
ask with openness
with softness
with the patience of tides
that return again and again

protect her boundaries
mirror them
honour them
never let her drown under obligation
never let her forget
she is allowed to rest

teach her to say *no*
and model it
show her how a mermaid
can turn her tail
and swim away from danger
from depletion
from the nets disguised as kindness

challenge misogyny
not alone
but together
two voices swell
three voices rise
a pod becomes a storm
and storms reshape coasts

share stories
the real ones
the unpolished ones
the ones you were told to hide
stories are shells
holding survival songs

celebrate her wins
loudly
publicly
unapologetically
because every victory for one woman
lifts the tide for all

check in
not once
but often
currents change
storms return
even the strongest swimmers
need another mermaid's hand
to break the surface

rest together
rest without guilt
rest as rebellion
rest as reclamation
rest as remembering
that ongoing struggle
requires ongoing tenderness

and above all

refuse to compete
refuse the myths
refuse to become the weapon
patriarchy hands you
refuse to harm another woman
to climb a ladder
built on her back

choose each other
over and over
as mermaids do
as long as there is ocean
as long as there is struggle
as long as there is hope

the mermaid code of solidarity

we swim together
through storms and stillness
no mermaid left behind
in any tide

we listen with the whole ocean
not just our ears
we honour each woman's truth
without doubt
without diminishing
without demanding proof

we believe her
before the world does
because the world is slow
to believe women
but mermaids are not

we guard each other's boundaries
as fiercely as our own
we do not let exhaustion
become a virtue
we do not let sacrifice
become a measure of worth

we say no
as an act of reclamation
we say yes
only when it uplifts
never when it erases

we lift each other's names
in rooms of power
we speak each other's brilliance
into tides that carry far

we share our maps
our survival strategies
our ways of navigating dangerous waters
nothing is hoarded
everything is offered

we do not compete
for the attention of waves
or the favour of sailors
or the myths that divide us
competition is the net
we refuse to swim into

we honour difference
as depth
we honour diversity
as strength
every mermaid's tail
is a different colour
every voice
a different current

we challenge harm
not with shame
but with truth
we do not let misogyny
hide in silence
or slip beneath the surface

we hold space
soft
expansive
brave
we make room
for grief
anger
healing
joy

we celebrate each victory
as if it lifts the entire sea
because it does

we rest
in pods
in circles
in quiet coves
because rest is resistance
and rest is how we rise again

we remember
that all mermaids
are daughters of the deep
bound by salt and struggle
bound by care
bound by the promise
to keep each other afloat

this is our code
our compass
our tide
our vow

we rise together
we lift the tide for all

remembering the shoreline

every mermaid knows
you must look after the shoreline
the meeting place
the breathing place
the place where you return
when tides run hard
so you can rise again
and help others rise too

take a long-breath steady
hold and exhale
breathe again
gentle waters drifting
there is a mermaid
gliding close

close your eyes
sink into the quiet
let the saltwater cradle you
let the currents soften your pulse
the way a lagoon settles
after wind has passed through

the mermaid rises
from the blue hush
her hair drifting like seagrass
her tail a slow shimmer
she moves with the ease
of someone born to water
someone who has never hurried
a single breath

she teaches you
how to breathe deep
how to follow the long exhale
down to that still quiet place
beneath the surface of yourself

feel the cool weight of ocean
resting over your shoulders
not heavy
just holding you
like country holding story
like tide holding moonlight

inhale
as though drawing water-light
through hidden inner gills
the kind your body only remembers
when calm finds you

exhale
as though releasing old storms
letting them drift away
into kelp forests
where green songs hum low
and patient

the mermaid circles
a slow gentle orbit
offering quiet
offering rest
she says without speaking
you belong to calm
you belong to breath
you belong to this water
that heals without demand

breathe again
long slow breaths
and longer still
until your bones remember
peace is not rare
only often misplaced

rest here
in the widening blue
in the drift
in the hush
held by mermaid calm
held by her presence
held by the gentle waters
within and around you

part three

mermaid notes

honouring

we honour
the first peoples of these lands and waters
their deep connection to country
their elders past and present
and the generations rising
sovereignty never ceded
this always was
and always will be
first nations country

mermaid story beginnings

once upon a time
a long time ago
in a far away place
in the arid zone
where red earth breathes heat
the sea retreats deep
and silence holds its own wisdom
three women meet

they were working
in different jobs
but all within social justice
community development
the slow fierce work
of making the world gentler
fairer
truer

they became friends
not in a sudden spark
but like small springs
finding each other
on desert soil
like tide meeting tide
recognising itself

in summer
they swam in the gulf with dolphins
before work
slipping into water
that held their laughter
their beginnings
their becoming

in cooler weather
they camped among sand dunes
where wind carved stories
into every curve
and horizon
held its long quiet breath

one identified birds
by flight
by call
by the soft flicker of wings
over saltbush and spinifex
naming each one
a small miracle
in a world that rarely paused
long enough to notice

they followed tracks
footprints of emu
kangaroo
lizard

patterns written in sand
that shifted with each hour
a language you learned
by kneeling close
by paying attention
by letting the land
set the pace

they walked wide lands
that asked nothing
but presence
lands that held memory
without judgement
lands that offered
stillness
and truth
to anyone willing to listen

they explored flora
tiny blooms
tenacious shrubs
plants that thrive
in heat and scarcity
their petals barely whispering
their leaves tough
their roots deep

learning resilience
from the earth itself
learning perseverance
from each drought shaped stem
learning that survival
is its own quiet defiance

and through it all
their friendship lived
like the changing light
on the gulf
like desert wind in the dunes
like birds that return
even after long journeys
finding each other
again and again
in every season

they travelled further
to more remote places
feeling the great quiet
around them
feeling grateful
for their opportunities
for the wild beauty
for the stories
they found together

eventually
they left that place
the origin point
of their friendship
and moved out
into different lives
different landscapes
different seasons

but the friendship endured
through the loss
of mutual friends
through illness
through distance
through everything
that shifts
breaks
rebuilds
a life

nowadays
they are all retired
from paid work

yet despite
the years that have passed
they are still activists
working toward equality
for women
and first nations people
they are still working
towards sustainability
for the environment
for social justice
for the future
they once dreamed of
under desert stars

two still volunteer
with the same fierce hearts
they carried in their twenties
hands still busy
still useful
still tending the world

and the other one
that is me

i create collage books
for children
cutting
shaping
weaving colour
and story
and care
into pages
for small hands
for young minds
for the next tide
of dreamers

and perhaps
this is where
the mermaid story begins

three women
in a dry land
learning early
that friendship
is its own ocean

three women
who swam with dolphins
and they had the audacity
to call themselves
mermaids

three women
who carried water
inside them
in a country
that knows thirst

three women
who refused silence
refused injustice
refused to stop caring

and all of us
still swimming
still shimmering
still believing
that friendship
and activism
and imagination
are currents
that can remake the world

this is the beginning
the first tide
the origin of everything
writing and creating

being a feminist

there is always a reaction
when i say the word out loud
some people nod
as if it is the most natural thing
a tide they have always known
others lean back
bristling like startled crabs
ready to pinch at anything
that challenges the shore

what more do you want for women
there is no pay gap
men can be victims too
why do you hate men

all i have done
is name myself
and suddenly the world thinks it knows
what i believe
what i demand
who i am

my definition is simple
i believe that girls and women
should have as many rights
as boys and men

that we deserve education
work
reproductive choices
safety
the vote
full participation
in the world we help carry

in the simplest of terms
i believe women should be equal
to men
no more
no less
just equal

when people ask
what more do you want
i tell them the truth
i want more women
to have access
to their hard earned rights
the ones fought for
by generations before us
the ones still withheld
from so many

what i want to do as a feminist
the *f* word
fierce
full
forward

i want girls growing up
to walk into their rights
without fear
without apology
i want to defend my own rights
because governments shift like sand
and tides can retreat
if we are not vigilant

as a young mother
i raised my sons
to cook
to clean
to care
to never rely on a woman
to absorb the labour of their lives

for my grandchildren
i want them unbound
by gender
free to step
into whatever worlds
they choose

the rights i have now
are gifts from the women
and the men who stood beside them
and i honour that lineage

i remember dale spender's words
feminism has fought no wars
killed no opponents
built no camps
starved no enemies
practised no cruelties
its battles have been
for education
for the vote
for working conditions
for safety in the streets
for child care
for social welfare
for rape crisis centres
for refuges
for justice

if someone says
i'm not a feminist
i ask
why
what's your problem

those words echo from 1980
forty five years ago
still sharp
still necessary

feminism is about lifting women
onto the same level as men
nothing radical about equality
except that the world fears it

being feminist
is being awake
being willing
being unafraid to act
being shaped
by other women
by their courage
by their words
by the tides they stirred

and here i swim
still reading
still learning
still fighting
still believing
in the power of the rising tide

mermaids

so the mermaids
their art story began not in the sea
but in the garden
mosaic on p v c pipes
glimmering in morning light
a small act of colour
against the ordinary

though truly
the first mermaid
was born from friendship
and a spark of defiance
a collaborative creation
to help two other artists
enter an exhibition
at a pretentious gallery
one that demanded artist biographies
as if art belonged only
to the approved

so we crafted a mermaid
and gave her my bio
we played the game
tiles shining brighter
than the self importance
in the room around us

after that
the next tide rose
an exhibition on the splendid hillside
at bethany wines
for the south australian living artists festival
mermaids singing in open air
above vines
along quarry stone
open sky
no pretence
only beauty
only truth

and then
before anyone knew
a pandemic could close the world
i took the sun bather mermaid
all the way to jindabyne
for the festival of light
her scales catching the alpine sun
as if she belonged there
in a landlocked dream
and on my way home
i left her at yandown
a gift to martina
happy dogs and a river
a reminder of a day on a boat
the bather sat gently among hills
overlooking the river
a mermaid travelling further
than i ever expected

then came illness
a tide that pulled me inward
so i mosaiced the house
tile by tile
a fantasy rock at first
then walls alive with colour
one mermaid for inner reflection
one diving deep
two playful ones twirling
on days when i could not

ten years
and every surface outside
became a shifting chorus
of tile
crockery
mirror
story
resilience

in the stillness of the pandemic
i created *andamooka anna*
and the murmuring mermaids
with two dear friends
a first book
woven from arid zone memory
friendship
and survival

then came the second
andamooka anna
and the amazing mermaids
bright
joyful
a celebration of making
friends collaborating
and remembering
that making together is a form of healing

now a third book
a romantasy
of *mermaid and merbird*
a love story unfolding
like tide meeting wind
and this book
this sea of misogyny
this vast ocean of truth
becomes the fourth
the deepest dive
the fiercest current
not because mermaids speak through me
no mysticism
no myth mistaken for prophecy
but because they inspire me
steady as tide
constant as salt
calling me back
to creation
to colour
to courage
to myself

and so the mermaids continue
mosaic and story
garden decoration and gallery floors
hillside vineyard and alpine light
house façade and printed page
they help me remember
that imagination is a kind of survival
and art is its own quiet medicine

Andamooka Anna and the Amazing Mermaids

ISBN 9780645558036   2024 June

Andamooka Anna and the Murmuring Mermaids

ISBN 9780645558074   2025 February

Mermaid and Merbird

ISBN 9781763563537   2026 February

Heather Gordon
artist, author children's book creator
Ngadjuri, Peramangk, Kaurna Country
Barossa Valley
Australia
https://heathergordon.com.au/